Andrea

A Lady of Letters

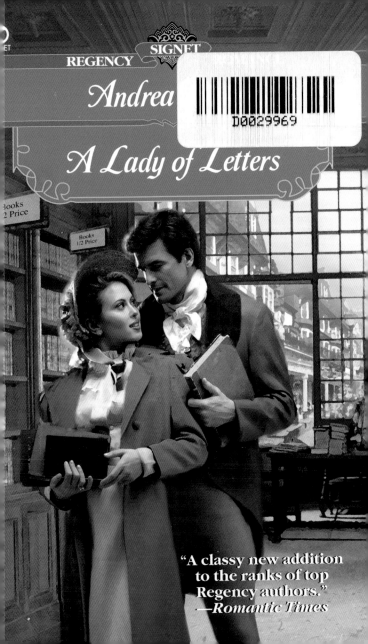

$4.99 U.S.
$6.99 CAN

ENCHANTING ROMANCES BY
ANDREA PICKENS

"The wonderful talent of
Andrea Pickens shines."
—*Romantic Times*

"This rising Regency
star will win a wide
audience for her
intriguing tale."
—*Romantic Times*

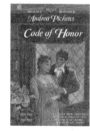

"A fresh, witty romp
with sparkling
dialogue and a dash
of danger."
—*Romantic Times*

ISBN 0-451-20170-1

"A finely wrought
love story featuring
an irresistible pair of
lovers who will melt
every reader's heart."
—*Romantic Times*

A MUTUAL AFFECTION

Augusta's mouth quirked upward in grim humor as she considered his words. "It does appear we know each other very well."

"Hmm. Very well, indeed." Sheffield was now standing quite close to her and could breathe in the faint scent of lavender and lemon from her person.

His mouth came down upon hers, with an urgency that nearly scorched both of their lips. She struggled to speak, but instead of allowing a word, he slipped his tongue deep inside her, twining with hers in a most intimate kiss. All attempt to elude his arms ceased, and with a low cry, she melted against his chest. Tentatively, she began to return his embrace, her fingers stealing up to brush the hard planes of his cheeks.

Her untutored response to him only stoked the fires of his passion. Wild thoughts flamed in his head as his hands pulled her close, molding every soft curve to his body. At that moment, he wanted nothing so much as to strip off all her clothes, lay her glorious body on the carpet before the crackling fire, and make passionate love to her, uniting them physically as one, just as they were joined in thought. . . .

A Lady
of Letters

Andrea Pickens

A SIGNET BOOK

SIGNET
Published by New American Library, a division of
Penguin Putnam Inc., 375 Hudson Street,
New York, New York 10014, U.S.A.
Penguin Books Ltd, 27 Wrights Lane,
London W8 5TZ, England
Penguin Books Australia Ltd, Ringwood,
Victoria, Australia
Penguin Books Canada Ltd, 10 Alcorn Avenue,
Toronto, Ontario, Canada M4V 3B2
Penguin Books (N.Z.) Ltd, 182–190 Wairau Road,
Auckland 10, New Zealand

Penguin Books Ltd, Registered Offices:
Harmondsworth, Middlesex, England

First published by Signet, an imprint of New American Library,
a division of Penguin Putnam Inc.

First Printing, October 2000
10 9 8 7 6 5 4 3 2 1

Chapter One

'Tis with great interest that I read your latest essay, sir. The ideas expressed are intriguing, to say the least, though I fear that they will hardly elicit any applause among the audience you wish to influence. In my experience, there are precious few people willing to admit to callousness and self-interest, however cleverly couched your chidings are. Nevertheless, your command of the written word, coupled with an originality of thought and razor wit, have won over at least one humble admirer to your singular intellect.

I must admit it has been years since anything has induced me to pick up a pen, but your words have sparked a few questions that perhaps you might have time to clarify for me. Might I be bold enough to ask whether you might consent to an occasional private correspondence? The passage of your work which has caused me to reflect on the nuances of its meaning begins with . . .

It was some time later that the Earl of Sheffield laid aside the sheets of paper and removed his gold-rimmed spectacles. With a rueful grimace he tucked them away in his desk drawer, thinking how utterly nonplussed his friends would be to see the Iron Adonis with such a foreign object in the grasp of his long fingers, rather than a bottle of brandy or a deck of cards—or the latest luscious opera dancer. No doubt even more shocking would be the fact that for the last several hours his thoughts had been preoccupied by matters considerably more complex than the upcoming sales at Tattersall's or the odds on whether Trowbridge would offer for the Wainwright chit before week's end.

His hand raked through his dark locks and another quick spasm tugged at the molded contours of his lips as he considered the truth of such a realization. Lord, had he really become such a shallow fribble as that? Oh, it was not that others saw him in such a light. On the contrary. In fact, he was quite aware that most of the *ton* regarded him with a respect that bordered on awe. No one dared question his opinions, lest they fall victim to his acerbic wit and end up skewered on his rapier-sharp tongue. Just as no one risked raising his ire, not with the prowess he displayed with his pistol at Manton's and his fists at Jackson's. That the scoundrel Montfort, a Captain Sharpe at cards who had ruined several green cubs, had provoked a duel and been sent to a deservedly early demise only seemed to have added to his stature.

He gave a resigned shake of his head. The more he thought about it, the more it seemed rather absurd. Young sprigs strove to emulate his sardonic stare as well as the knot of his cravat, while more ladies than he cared to count vied for his attention. His own circle of acquaintances was no less adoring, for despite his penchant for occasional fits of temper or practical jokes that went too far, he was admired as a generous host, bruising sportsman, and loyal friend. Even the highest sticklers curried his favor, excusing his rather rakish reputation because, along with his wealth and title, he was accorded to be a gentleman of impeccable manners and taste.

But of late, he found that his own judgment of himself was far less flattering.

With a heavy sigh he rose and went to the sideboard and poured himself a stiff brandy. Though he returned to his chair, a certain restlessness of spirit had his eyes wandering from the blazing fire in the hearth to the rows of leatherbound books lining the heavy oak shelves. He had used to enjoy cracking their spines, he mused. There was a time the ideas and insights had sparked a flame in his breast nearly as bright and lively as the ones he watched now. How had he let it die out?

Had he merely been lazy? he asked. After a moment, his mouth compressed in a thin line. No, self-indulgent was more apt. The boisterous gaiety of shared spirits, the sweet softness of a willing lady, the frisson of excitement at the turn of a card—all had turned his attention from serious matters that required more effort.

It had come so easily, the ability to excel at the sorts of things his friends held in such high regard— gambling, riding, shooting, cutting a swath through the ladies. He had been seduced by their admiration, drunk with the notion of his own consequence. His fingers came up to rub at his temples. Lord, he had to admit he had made some foolish choices in his youth. And now he was paying for them, for he found his life was becoming an interminable bore. It was flat, smooth, without any unexpected edge to cut his ennui. Another Season was fast approaching, along with his thirty-second birthday, and what did it offer? The idea of yet another round of carousing with his friends, or racing his curricle to Bath on a wager, or even a visit to his latest mistress left him feeling nothing but a disquieting coldness in the pit of his stomach.

Sheffield fingered his pen as his gaze fell to the finished letter on his blotter. An amused chuckle stole forth. *Firebrand* was how the anonymous writer signed his essay. It was an apt moniker, indeed, given the heated words. He hoped that his missive, to be delivered to the man's publisher in the morning, would reach the mysterious author and be given the favor of a reply. Perhaps it wasn't too late to rekindle an interest in something deeper than a glass of brandy.

On impulse, he reached out and scribbled a final signature. He had been debating whether to reveal his own identity, but was loath to have "Firebrand" judge him by reputation alone. As he regarded the name staring up from the paper it seemed much more fitting to sign his missive this way.

He hoped the fellow would appreciate the humorous touch.

Lady Augusta Hadley choked down a burble of laughter.

"Gus!"

She quickly folded the paper and stuffed it into her desk as her younger sister flew into the little room she used as her study. "Do slow down, Marianne. Mama would no doubt swoon over such an unladylike entrance," she admonished, though her smile took any sting out of her words.

"Oh, I am heartily sick of being all that is proper," answered the young lady, dropping onto the comfortable wing chair with a flounce that sent her elegant gown into a welter of wrinkles.

"Heresy from the Goddess of Greenfield," murmured Augusta.

Marianne stuck out her tongue. "If you, of all people, dare repeat that sickening sobriquet out loud I shall plant you a facer!" She tucked her dainty feet up under her skirts and let her chin fall on her arms. "Really, I do wish we could steal out for a gallop through the fields. All these morning calls with Mama are tedious to the extreme."

Augusta's brow arched upward. "I thought you were enjoying yourself."

"Well, I am," admitted Marianne. "I do like the balls and routs and such, but I am never allowed a moment to myself. You on the other hand—"

"I, on the other hand, am firmly on the shelf. Mama

has finally shown signs of giving up trying to threaten, beg or force me into some semblance of proper behavior. Her attention is now firmly focused on you—and with good reason." She surveyed her sister's blonde curls, cherubic features, and diminutive figure. Even the most critical eye would be hard-pressed to find fault with the girl. Cornflower-blue eyes radiated a winsome innocence, while lips as plump as cherries— Good lord, she admonished herself, she was in danger of waxing as ridiculous as the besotted young viscount who had dubbed Marianne the Goddess of Greenfield in a fit of rapture after his first dance. Still, there was no denying that the girl was a Diamond of the First Water, with any number of eligible suitors already dangling on her sleeve although the Season had hardly begun. "You have, as Mama would say, taken rather well."

Marianne scrunched up those perfect lips. "If you made even the slightest effort to attract attention, you should leave me in the dust, Gus. I wish I had your height and those glorious cheekbones. Instead, I am short and have a plumpness to my face that reminds me of a squirrel. And I wish I had your brains—"

Augusta grimaced. "*Never* let Mama hear you say such a thing. I am enough of a trial as it is. Two such daughters would send her into permanent decline. Besides, you are hardly a ninny, my dear. You simply know when to keep your mouth shut, which is something I have never managed to learn."

"Or care about."

"Well, I suppose that might have something to do with it."

Both of them laughed.

"Seriously, Gus," continued her sister after a bit, "why is it you are so set against making yourself agreeable to the many gentlemen who would show an interest if you gave them half a chance?"

"You know very well why," she muttered. "You are

content with the idea of a husband and children and a household to run, but it would not suit for me."

"Surely there are men who would appreciate your keen intellect, and not seek to keep you from expressing your views."

"Hah! If you think any man would countenance my opinions, especially if he knew that—" She swallowed hard. "I mean, *you* may know that I am capable of stringing two coherent thoughts together, but the fact is, in public I stutter and natter like a veritable peagoose, which, combined with my gangly height and angular features, is hardly likely to set any gentleman's heart to flutter." She made a show of rearranging the papers on her cluttered desk. "Truly, Marianne, I am well content as I am. Don't you, too, start asking me to change."

Her sister bit her lip. "I meant no such thing, Gus, you know I didn't. It's just that . . ." Her words trailed off with a sigh.

"Come now, let's have no long faces." Augusta quickly changed the subject. "What was it you were in such a hurry to tell me?"

"Oh, as to that, Mama was wondering if you might attend the Crestleighs' ball with me tonight. She is having one of her megrims and wishes to stay in bed. Of course, if you do not wish to, I should be happy to stay at home as well."

"And forgo an evening of watching Stonehill whisper insipid verses in your ear and Evershaw try not to tread on your toes as he gazes like a mooncalf into your eyes? How could I ever pass up such entertainment?"

"They mean well, poor things," Marianne said, trying to stifle a giggle. "You don't mind, then?"

"I am looking forward to it—why, just yesterday I purchased a turban for exactly this sort of occasion."

Marianne rolled her eyes. "Rather, wear your figured emerald silk and see just who needs a chaperone." On that note, she picked herself up and left as precipitously as she had entered.

Augusta gave a little shake of her head as the door fell shut. What an odd notion her sibling had taken into that lovely head of hers, to imagine that she might be of the slightest attraction to the opposite sex. It was just as well it was utter nonsense. She hadn't time to waste fending off unwanted suitors, not if she was to get done all the things that she needed to in the next few months. Already she was a bit behind schedule to meet her next deadline.

And then there was the real reason she had agreed to leave the comfortable environs of Greenfield Manor and endure the distractions of a Season in Town. Good Lord, she hadn't even had a chance to begin looking into that, she thought grimly. Perhaps tonight would provide the opportunity to start asking a few discreet questions. Her brow furrowed slightly as she turned her mind to formulating a plan for her investigation. That it would take luck as well as logic to succeed had already occurred to her. Being a female was going to be a great hindrance in this matter, but with Jamison's help, they might manage to discover what was needed.

The chiming of the clock on the mantel chased such thoughts away for the time being. If she applied herself, she decided on looking at the notes before her, she might be able to finish another page of her writing before it was time to dress for the evening.

But first, she would finish that interesting letter that had just arrived from Pritchard's office.

Sheffield strolled through the packed ballroom, noting with wry exasperation that at least four young cubs fresh from the country were wearing the same burgundy and charcoal striped waistcoat that he had sported last week at Audley's ball. Making a mental note to have his valet destroy it at once, he took a glass of champagne from a passing waiter and swept his gaze over the latest array of young ladies to make their come-out.

After a long look, his mouth tugged down at the corners. Hell's teeth, was he really getting so old? Why, the chits looked like mere children! And no doubt their thoughts would match their smiling faces—bland, agreeable, scrubbed of all hint of originality. He drained his glass and turned in search of another.

"What? None of the newest Incomparables meet with your august approval? I had thought the blonde, at least, might catch your eye."

"Really, Fitz, when have you known me to consider ravishing little girls?" he muttered, moving restlessly toward a corner of the room. "Innocents have little appeal to me." His current unsettled mood led him to be more acerbic than usual. "Take the blonde you mentioned—I wager there is not one word worth hearing that would come from that rosebud mouth. And most assuredly she would have no idea of how to make any other part of her anatomy more . . . interesting."

His friend gave a muffled guffaw.

"No," he continued. "The trouble far outweighs any sort of reward one might expect. I shall stick to more mature ladies, who at least offer some sort of recompense for having to endure their inane chatter."

The two of them had paused beside a towering arrangement of potted palms woven with a cascade of ivy spilling from the terra cotta containers. The earl's friend finished his drink and gave one more glance around the room. "I fear you are right. This evening promises to be a dead bore. Nothing here but scheming mamas looking to make a match. Care to join me for a bottle at White's? I might also decide to try my luck at that new gaming hell off Pall Mall."

Sheffield slapped at one of the long fronds brushing the shoulder of his immaculately tailored evening jacket. "Perhaps I will join you later," he said curtly.

The other man's brow furrowed a bit at the earl's sharp tone, then he simply shrugged and backed off through the swirl of dancing couples.

Sheffield's attention turned once again to the crowded ballroom. Somehow, the violins were starting to sound like the screech of an owl, the deep bass of the violas no more harmonious than the lowing of a cow. The mingled laughter rang shrill to his ears and the scent of the flowers seemed unbearably cloying. His mood grew even darker as he rued the force of habit that had caused him to dress with great care and come out, even though his inclination had been to retreat to his library and begin perusing the sheaf of articles he had lately gathered on the state of child labor. Firebrand's essay had piqued him to look into the matter and it was proving a most interesting subject.

Abandoning his usual nonchalant manner, he turned abruptly on his heel—only to collide with a another figure nearly hidden in the wave of fronds. A goodly amount of lemonade splashed onto his cravat and dribbled down the front of his waistcoat. As he watched the sticky liquid turn the embroidered cream silk a sickly shade of yellow, the look of faint ennui on his countenance dissolved into an expression of undisguised anger.

"Damnation." The words slipped out of his mouth, just loudly enough to be heard. His eyes came up from the ruined garment only to find the subject of his curse was a female. Still, his ire was roused enough that he continued on, despite the look of shock on her ashen face. "Cannot you look where you are going?" he snapped. Taking in the spectacles perched on her nose, he added, "Or do you require even more than four eyes to avoid being a menace to Society?"

"I . . . I . . ." she stammered.

"Eyes, not eye. Plural, not singular. Try keeping them open!" He knew it was hardly fair, using such biting sarcasm on one who clearly would not have the wits nor the backbone to fight back, but he found he couldn't restrain himself.

The young lady drew in a sharp intake of breath.

The earl's eyes pressed closed. Hell's teeth, that was all he needed! No doubt the chit was about to dissolve in a fit of hysterics and the whole room would know of this ridiculous incident. Why hadn't he reined in his temper—

"Pompous ass."

His lids flew open. "What!" She had spoken so softly that he wasn't sure he had heard her correctly.

The young lady's hand flew to her mouth, as if it could belatedly snatch the words back. But instead of mumbling some distraught apology, she sucked in another breath and went on. "And a vulgar one as well. How dare you speak of the young ladies here as if they were . . . idiots."

With a start he realized she must have overheard his previous words. His lips compressed. He was certainly not showing to advantage in this whole mess, but somehow the knowledge only goaded him to further rudeness.

"They *are* idiots. *All* of them." By the way his disdainful gaze slowly traveled the full length of her person as he spoke, he made it quite clear she was not excluded from the sweeping generalization.

She gasped, whether in horror or outrage he wasn't sure. Then he looked through the glass lenses of her spectacles and caught sight of the storm of indignation swirling in a sea of hazel frothed with specks of gold. Oh, it was anger all right, nearly as tempestuous as his own. For a moment he regarded the face glaring up at him. Or rather straight at him, for she could hardly be described as diminutive. She was not quite so young as the other misses gathered under the watchful eyes of their chaperones. Aside from the intriguing eyes, which showed no lack of expression, her cheekbones were high and prominent, her mouth a little wider than conventional beauty allowed, giving her features a certain unique character. She was not exactly pretty, but . . . interesting, especially now that a flush of color had returned to her cheeks and several tendrils the color of wheat at harvest time had escaped the simple arrangement of her hair and fallen to accentuate the graceful curve of her neck.

By now, she had finally managed to think of a reply to his mocking statement. "Well, why are you complaining, then? I . . . I thought that was what men wanted—ladies who are idiots."

He was rather surprised she hadn't simply turned tail by now and slunk away. Never had he encountered a female who dared raise her voice to him—or any gentleman—much less mutter unflattering epithets. She was certainly exhibiting an unusual spirit to go along with her looks, he granted. However, right now, such singular behavior was only serving to fan the flames of his temper.

His dark brows drew together in a manner calculated to appear intimidating. "Ah, but what we want are *charming* idiots," he countered. "*Well-behaved* idiots. Not ones whose tongues are sharper than their wits and who have no better common sense than to create a hoydenish scene in a crowded ball room." His gaze raked over her once again, taking in the defiant tilt of her chin, the unladylike scowl. "With such lack of restraint, not to speak of clumsiness, no wonder you have reached an advanced age with no success in snaring a husband."

Her color deepened to a bright red. She stood utterly tongue-tied for several moments, her mouth opening then shutting without a sound coming forth. Then, with the half-empty glass still clutched in her hand, she whirled and disappeared behind the trees.

Sheffield's mouth thinned into a tight line. That had been needlessly cruel, he thought with a twinge of conscience. It wasn't at all like him to act in such an ungentlemanly fashion, but somehow the chit had caused the frayed ends of his patience to snap. He supposed he ought to follow her and make some apology. He had been wrong to let his damnable temper cause him to lose control. If he were honest with himself, she had not been entirely to blame for the unfortunate incident. After all, his words *had* been rather harsh and, as she had put it, rather vulgar.

The young lady—for despite his cutting words, she did not appear to be entirely on the shelf—didn't deserve to be so ruthlessly skewered for trying to defend those of her sex. She had shown more grit than he had ever expected in a female, even though she had been no match in trying to cross verbal swords with him.

His lips suddenly twitched as he recalled she hadn't been totally unable to express herself. Why, she had called him a pompous ass! A glance down at his ruined garment caused another wry grimace. He could almost believe the chit had done it on purpose, but that would most likely be according her too much credit for clever retribution. At least, she had made his decision on how to pass the rest of the evening a simple one. He had no choice but to return to his townhouse and change out of the sticky mess. And given the way the evening had been progressing, the thought of reading by the fire seemed even more appealing.

Odious coxcomb!

Augusta took a deep breath and tried to settle her seething emotions. Why was it she seemed to need ink and paper in front of her to compose her thoughts properly? From her pen, the right words seemed to run with an exuberant spontaneity while when in the presence of strangers they tripped on her tongue, tangling themselves in such a way as to make her sound, well, idiotic, if she spoke at all. Only the fact that she had been absolutely furious over the insult to Marianne had allowed her to make such a bold assault on the gentleman before her natural reticence reasserted itself. That she had turned and fled without coming up with even a halfway pithy retort to his insult made her annoyance with herself even greater.

If she were going to make an ass of herself in public, why couldn't she at least be a clever ass?

She fetched a fresh glass of lemonade, still fuming over the incident. Gentleman indeed! The Earl of Sheffield appeared to be even worse than his reputation suggested. Her own brief experience certainly corroborated certain whispers that he was hot-tempered and arrogant, a jaded rake, puffed up with a sense of his own importance.

Out of the corner of her eye, she caught sight of his tall, elegantly dressed figure among the throng of milling couples. He was undeniably handsome, she grudgingly allowed, and moved with an easy natural grace which she wished her long, gawky limbs could emulate. But the look of sardonic boredom on his chiseled lips as his gaze moved over the crowd only reaffirmed her impression that he was the most insufferable man she had ever met.

"Oh dear, whatever is wrong, Gus?" whispered Marianne, leaning close to take the glass from her sister's hands.

"What makes you think anything is wrong," she answered through gritted teeth.

Marianne turned to smile prettily at her latest dance partner, remarking that she had changed her mind and would prefer ratafia punch to lemonade. As the young man hurried off, she took Augusta by the arm and moved out of the hearing of two stout matrons sitting nearby. "Your cheeks are exactly the shade of red they get when Uncle Charles remarks that ladies should not read certain books lest they confuse our feeble minds."

Augusta allowed a tight smile. "I'm surprised they aren't even redder, given the provocation." She took a deep breath. "Pay it no heed, I just . . . bumped into a most unpleasant gentleman, that is all."

Marianne looked surprised, but the expression on her sister's face made her think better of pursuing the matter. After a moment she sought to change the subject. "Was that really the Earl of Sheffield you were conversing with near the refreshment room? I was not aware that you were acquainted with him."

"I am not acquainted with him. Nor do I wish to be. In fact, if I never see that arrogant, insufferable man again I shall be well pleased. And I can safely assume he feels the same way." At her sister's startled expression, she went on to explain. "We were not conversing. We were trading insults, though I fear he got much the better of me." Her lips compressed into a grim smile. "But at least I managed to dampen His Lordship's overweening pride with over half a glass of lemonade."

Marianne let out a horrified gasp. "You didn't! Oh, Gus, no wonder he was upset. Why, he is accorded to be one of the most fashionable men in Town. All the young dandies seek to copy his dress—"

"Well then, waistcoats streaked with a rather ghastly shade of yellow should be all the crack next week."

"Gus!"

"It wasn't as if I did it on purpose." She paused a fraction. "Not exactly."

Her sister had gone rather pale. "It is said he is a very powerful man, one you should not wish to make an enemy of."

Augusta's chin came up a fraction. "It doesn't matter. He was unforgivably rude about all the young misses here, and you in particular."

"Me!" Marianne looked totally confused now. "Why, he doesn't know me!"

"Precisely."

Any further conversation on the matter was cut off by the return of Mr. Darby and another young man who had danced the first set with Marianne. Their offer to escort the two sisters in to supper was accepted and the four of them followed the crowd heading toward the tables heaped with all manner of delicacies.

Augusta couldn't help but notice that the earl was coming in her direction. When it looked for one horrible moment as if he might pause, she drew her brows together and shot him a black look that she hoped was just as intimidating as the one he had given her earlier. To her great satisfaction, he passed by without so much as a nod of acknowledgment.

Sheffield watched the four young people pass. No wonder the lady had been upset, he thought. The blonde was obviously a friend—no, on closer observation, it appeared likely they were related, though the younger girl was more conventionally pretty than his antagonist. That made his crude comments even worse, though it hadn't been *his* fault she had been skulking in the greenery, eavesdropping on a decidedly private conversation between two gentlemen.

Still, he should have known better than to voice such sentiments in mixed company. It was a measure of how out of kilter he was feeling these days, to make such a silly error in judgment. He knew he should force himself to proffer an apology, but the presence of the two young men caused his jaw to clench. He'd be damned if he'd make any more of a cake of himself tonight by exposing the ridiculous affair to the ears of those young pups. It would be all over the clubs before midnight!

He would do the pretty the next time he saw her.

Or perhaps he would get lucky and never have to lay eyes on the offending chit again.

Chapter Two

. . . I hope that this brief overview has served to offer some clarification of my thoughts concerning the nature of a society that permits child labor. Your questions, despite your assertions to the contrary, were most thoughtful and showed an inquisitiveness and openness to new ideas that I find sadly lacking in most supposedly educated men of today. You may trust that I found answering them by no means an onerous chore. Indeed, I am gratified by your interest and should be happy to engage in a regular exchange of letters, as you suggest, and pursue further explorations of ideas and ideals. As to that, I believe you will find my next essay even more interesting.

> *Yours sincerely, etc.*
> *Firebrand*

Sheffield carefully folded the thick sheets of paper and tucked them into the top drawer of his desk. Fresh from an early morning ride in Hyde Park, he found the letter that had awaited his return even more exhilarating than the rush of fresh air in his face. At last a chance to exercise his mind without fear of ridicule or censure! Not that he cared a whit what others thought, but there were precious few of his acquaintances who would understand his current restlessness, or not think him a candidate for Bedlam for turning the pages of aught but the betting book at their club.

He sighed. And the sort of gentlemen who might be capable of rational conversation were also out of the question, for they would no doubt have a preconceived notion of the limited mental capacities of a rake and a libertine and refuse to take him seriously.

His crop slapped against the polished leather of his Hessians as he rose and walked toward the breakfast room of his townhouse. No, this was perfect, he thought, a smile of satisfaction spreading across his face. The idea of it was incredibly liberating—he could wax philosophic in perfect anonymity, to be judged only on the merits of his ideas, not the notoriety of his past actions or the trappings of his pedigree. Any praise would be deserved, just as would be any chidings or ridicule, though he doubted such an intellectual as Firebrand would resort to the latter. The fellow had been kind in commending him for his first cautious questions and the earl found himself wanting to rise a notch higher in the fellow's esteem, perhaps even earn the man's respect for his own capabilities. It would be a real challenge, for the standards would be high, but it was one which he looked forward to.

A packet from Pritchard & Sons containing their latest pamphlet lay by his teacup. Ignoring the sideboard set with steaming shirred eggs, fresh scones, and a platter of Yorkshire ham, he tore open the wrappings, his appetite whetted for ideas rather than any meal. His impatient fingers paged back the thin newsprint cover and he began to devour the words.

It was nearly midday before the earl had finished reading and rereading the long discourse. With a shake of his head, he sat back in his chair, full of admiration for both the powerful thoughts and the elegant turn of the phrases. It was rather like being skewered by a jeweled sword, he thought wryly, glitter and color disguising a lethal sharpness. Why, the language was so richly wrought one could almost forget that the words were a slashing attack on the complacency of the *ton*. He imagined there would be more than a few howls of outrage in the clubs tonight, as well as perhaps a few muted agreements.

Several of the references to other books had caught his attention. He consulted his pocketwatch and decided he had just enough time to make their purchase before meeting up with Broadhurst and Wilton at Tattersall's.

Augusta's brow puckered as she looked over the notes in front of her. Each small pile was carefully sorted and arranged to document a certain facet of her argument, but on the last few ideas, she was still in need of a better reference. Muttering darkly under her breath, she put her pen down. There was no getting around it, she would have to pick up a few more volumes for her research.

Marianne's head came up from the copy of *La Belle Assemblée* she was perusing. "What was that you said?"

"Nothing."

"Oh yes, you did. You said 'damnation' under your breath." She repressed a chuckle. "Pray, do be careful Mama doesn't hear you, else she will sink into a fit of vapors that could last a week."

Augusta heaved a sigh. "I am not quite so addle-pated as that. It's just that I had planned to spend the afternoon working and now I find I must go out. Do you wish to come along?"

Her sister shook her head. "I am to go out for a drive with Lord Symonds later and I should never have enough time to make myself ready. Besides, I want to finish choosing a style for the new ball gowns Mama wishes me to have." She paused for a moment to regard Augusta's profile and the way the light filtering in from the window highlighted strong lines of her face and the golden flecks in her hazel eyes, now sparking with a flare of annoyance. "Come look at this one. It would look marvelous on you, what with your height and figure."

Augusta brushed away a loose tendril of hair. "I have more than enough gowns," she said absently as she rummaged in her desk for some other papers.

"Yes, all of which look perfectly dreadful since you paid not the slightest attention to their cut or color and let Mrs. Huston do as she wished."

"Mrs. Huston has been making my dresses since I was a child," replied Augusta.

"That is precisely my point. The woman is a dear old thing, but she has no eye for how you should be attired."

"It hardly matters. It is *you* who need be concerned over such things, not me."

Marianne's brow creased. "You are wrong, you know. I can see that gentlemen take notice of you, and if you would give them even half a chance . . ." Her finger traced over the elegant picture in front of her. "Why, I couldn't help but notice that even Lord Sheffield continued to follow you with his eyes the other night, and everyone says he is a man whose interest does not usually lie with young misses."

"Hah!" Augusta gave a snort. "He was merely trying to decide whether he could get away with pitching me headfirst over the balcony into the garden fountain. And anyway, the interest of *that* sort of man would hardly be flattering. He is exactly the sort of gentleman I find abhorrent—vain, shallow, and self-absorbed."

"But surely there are others who you find of some interest," persisted Marianne. "You seem to enjoy the conversation of Lord Harwich."

"He, at least, has a sensible mind lurking beneath those carefully arranged curls," she allowed. "But . . ." She finished scribbling a list of things she needed and stood up.

Seeing that the discussion was at an end, Marianne returned to her original objective. "Why don't you let me have some gowns made up for you as well. I know

exactly what would suit you, and Madame Celeste's
workmanship is superb."

Augusta stuffed the piece of paper in her pocket.
"Oh, very well, if it pleases you." She gave another
sigh. "Enjoy your outing. No doubt Mama will have
a host of errands for me, so I shall be not be back
for ages."

Indeed, she was not in the best of moods by the
time she arrived at Hatchard's. Not only had the vari-
ous stops for her mother taken more time than she
had expected, but the conversation with Marianne had
stirred up a number of unsettling feelings. It wasn't as
if she were entirely immune to the attractions of the
opposite sex, she mused, or that she wished to spend
the rest of her days alone or as the doting spinster
aunt to Marianne's future brood of children. It was
just that those few gentleman she knew who possessed
a brain had little else to recommend them, while those
whose other attributes might have caused her pulse to
quicken always proved a bigger disappointment, what
with their lack of wit or common sense. In short, all
of them left her feeling lukewarm at best.

Other ladies, Marianne included, seemed to have no
trouble finding men they could wax enthusiastic over.
Were her own standards really so impossibly high?

The carriage rolled to a halt and she forced aside
such glum thoughts. Leaving her maid at the front of
the shop to search out a few popular titles for Marianne, Augusta made her way among the tall shelves
to hunt for an obscure work from one of the French
philosophers. Twenty minutes later her arms were full
of books, but the one she desired still had not been
located. Eyes glued to the very top row of offerings,
she rounded the corner in a hurry, anxious to find it
and be done.

Whoomph.

The collision nearly knocked her off her feet, but
she managed to grab hold of the edge of the polished
wood shelf. The gentleman was not so fortunate. He

was sent crashing to the floor, along with the assorted volumes that Augusta had been carrying. One rather large book caught him a sharp clip on the head as he made to sit up.

"Hell and damnation," he muttered, rubbing at his brow. When his eyes came up, another word followed, though he spoke it low enough that she couldn't quite make it out. There was no mistaking the look of annoyance in his glare, however. *"You!"* he growled. "I seem to be cursed with the misfortune of making your acquaintance yet again. Have your parents considered locking you up in a barn, as a favor to Society? You are clumsier than the proverbial bull in a china shop."

"The only curses seem to be coming from *your* unbridled mouth, sir. Perhaps it is *you* who should be locked up in a stall, given such barnyard manners." Her feelings were already in an agitated state, and his untempered rudeness caused a wave of anger to wash away her usual shyness. Really, how dare the insufferable man keep implying that the blame for these mishaps was all hers.

A slight flush came to the earl's cheeks as he rose to his feet and carefully brushed the dust from his immaculate navy merino jacket. He looked as if to say something, but Augusta pointedly turned her back on him and began to gather up her books as if he didn't exist. When she straightened, he was still standing there, regarding her with a look that made no attempt to hide his ire at her deliberate snub. His gaze raked down from her slightly disheveled hair, to the prim neckline of her gown, to the pile of leatherbound volumes in her arms. A snort of derision came from his curled lips as he surveyed the titles. "Your father ought to send a more capable person to do his errands," he sneered. "You really should stay in the section with horrid novels—much more the thing for your type of flighty female."

She knew she shouldn't bother to respond to his gibe, but she couldn't restrain herself. "These books are for *me,* sir, not my father or any other male relative."

He gave a bark of laughter. "Hah! You may leave off trying to convince me of that farrididdle. Somehow I doubt that sewing and sketching and whatever other inane things you ladies learn in the schoolroom have quite prepared your intelligence—such as it is—for these works. They may be in French, but they are not flowery snippets of romantic nonsense. You are wasting your money and your time. Why, I'd be willing to wager a goodly sum that you won't get past the first page."

"A fool and his money are soon parted," she retorted, gratified to see his eyes narrow in further irritation. "And what do you think—that winning a fortune at cards, racing a curricle down St. James's Place at midnight in the buff, and bedding other men's wives qualifies *you* as intelligent?" she went on, heedless of what dangerous ground she was now treading on.

There was a moment of ominous silence. "Have a care, Miss," he said softly. "If you were a man I should be tempted to call you out for such words."

"If I were a man, I imagine I should be tempted to accept." She paused a fraction. "But women have infinitely more sense than to wave pistols at each other on account of some momentary fit of pique." With that, she shouldered her way past him and walked quickly toward the front of the store.

"Now that, my dear, is the proper way to make an exit," murmured Sheffield under his breath as he watched her walk away. His anger was slowly giving way to a grudging admiration. Once again, an awkward situation had prompted less than exemplary behavior from him, yet this time, she had not fled in tongue-tied embarrassment but rather had parried his sharp words with equally cutting ones of her own. Indeed, she had accounted for herself quite credibly, her setdowns showing a quickness and a clever-

ness he would never have suspected from their initial
encounter.

She was obviously not as bird-witted as he had first
imagined, though he wasn't sure he quite believed her
assertion that the books were for herself. They were
difficult going. Of that he was well aware, for several
of them were ones he had been struggling to make
sense of for the past week. His lips quirked. Perhaps
he should discover who she was so he could arrange
to meet her father or brother. If they had half the
spark that she did, it might prove interesting to culti-
vate the acquaintance, though, judging by her manner
of dress, it didn't promise to be a family of any consequence. However, he might actually discover someone
he could share an intelligent conversation with.

The earl carefully rearranged the folds of his cravat
and brushed the minute wrinkles from his fawn
breeches. The girl was certainly developing an unfortunate knack for making him look bad—in every respect. He was suddenly aware that not only had he
forgotten to tender an apology to her for the other
evening but that he had compounded his earlier trans-
gressions with an even worse account of himself today.
It wasn't as if it mattered a whit what some unfashionably dressed chit thought of him, but his honor as a
gentleman demanded that he at least offer some words
of regret for his unsavory language. A lady, no matter
how provoking, should not be subjected to such words.
After locating the book for which he had come, he
tucked it under his arm and returned to the front of
the store, determined to get the thing over with.

There was no sign of her. He turned to the clerk
hovering near his elbow. "Another customer was just
here and purchased a number of books. Do you know
who she is?"

"M-Miss Hadley?" stammered the fellow.

Hadley. His brows drew together. "Farnum's daughter?" he demanded.

The clerk nodded. "Y-yes, my lord. She comes here quite often."

Good Lord, he thought, as his book was taken away to be wrapped. Edwin Hadley's sister. Now it was not merely honor that required him to make an apology, but something even more important.

Try as she might to focus her attention on the printed page, her thoughts kept turning to the lean face, the full, mobile, lips curved in a look of distaste while the mocking blue eyes made no attempt to hide a look of utter disapproval.

As if she cared what the insufferable man thought of her!

Augusta snapped the book shut and began to pace her small study. This time, at least, she hadn't made a complete hash of defending herself from his cutting words. In fact, she realized with a start, her ripostes had sallied forth, unbidden, before she had had a chance to think about what she had been saying. Not only that, they had actually pricked the man's over-weening pride. Though it might have been foolhardy to risk making an enemy of such a man as the Earl of Sheffield, it had been worth it to see the look of surprise, then outrage that spread over his features.

It was a shame those features were so riveting to look at.

The tumble of dark locks, worn longer than was fashionable, and arched brows only accentuated the depth of color to his eyes. Not a soft, languid blue but a rich cerulean plummeting to shades of slate when his ire was raised—a state with which she was growing quite familiar.

The angular planes of his face emphasized the sense of chiseled strength that radiated from his person. No matter his other faults, weakness of character did not appear to be one of them. It was interesting, too, that the hardness in his face did not have the look of calcu-lated coldness or cruelty. Though it was hard to explain, she sensed that his anger might appear razor-sharp, yet was somehow a bit blunted around the edge.

And he was not stupid. His quick tongue and reputation for acerbic wit proved that, though she rather doubted that his thoughts ever ventured beyond issuing scathing setdowns. After all, if rumors were true, he spent all his time in idle pursuit of pleasure. His luck at the gaming tables was legendary, as was his prowess at sport . . . and seduction. More than a few whispers during the interminable morning calls she was forced to make with her mother and sister had reached her ears concerning his all too obvious charms.

She found herself thinking about the sensual curve of that broad mouth, and what it would feel like to have them pressed against her own—

What in heaven's name was she thinking of, to entertain such improper, not to speak of absurd, notions! Why, she loathed the man, and it was clear he felt the same way about her. But it seemed her body was intent on betraying her intellect, feeling a perverse attraction to the most unsuitable choice imaginable. Her hands flew to her cheeks. They were hot to the touch. Perhaps she was coming down with a bout of fever, for only a sudden illness could account for such a delirium.

Or perhaps she had merely stepped too close to the blazing fire.

She retreated to her desk and took out a leather journal from the locked top drawer. If she could not concentrate on her research, she could at least begin to review her notes on what had taken place during the past several months in the area surrounding Greenfield Manor. In a matter of minutes all thoughts of mesmerizing blue eyes and masculine smiles were gone, replaced by the chilling images of three children, all of whom had disappeared without a trace.

Her rapid scribbling ceased only when a soft knock

came at the door. "Still at work? Don't forget that you promised to attend the Loudens' ball with us tonight." Marianne sat down on the comfortable sofa, her face still flushed a becoming pink from the jaunt in the park. "I thought you had finished your essay for Mr. Pritchard."

Augusta nibbled at the tip of her pen. "I have. It is now time to turn my attention to the plight of our neighbors. Mrs. Roberts asked for my help and I mean to do my best to discover what is going on."

Marianne's expression turned to one of concern. "I don't like the idea of your getting involved in such things. It might be dangerous. Why not write to Papa? He will think of something."

"Papa is in Vienna and not likely to return for months. There is nothing he can do."

"Then speak to the magistrate."

"Squire Hillhouse!" Her brows arched up. "That bumbling fool won't lift a finger to help a mere tenant," she said in some disgust. "Besides, he couldn't unravel a crime if the evidence were twined around his bulbous nose and tied in a pretty bow."

Marianne brought her knees up to her chin. "If only Edwin were here to advise—"

"Well, he is not," said Augusta rather sharply. "So it is up to me." On seeing her sister's stricken expression she bit her lip. "I'm sorry, lamb." she said gently. "I miss him terribly, too."

Marianne swallowed hard. "How do you mean to start?"

Augusta gestured to the open pages of her journal. "First, I am compiling a list of all the gentry with residences within twenty miles of the village."

"Are you really so sure it is someone who lives nearby, and that he is . . . one of us? I mean, couldn't it have been the work of a band of ruffians merely passing through? I have read of such things."

She shook her head. "It is unlikely. I have had Jamison make inquiries in all the neighboring towns and there are no other reports of children gone missing, plus the time between the occurrences makes the chance of it being a random act quite slim." She took something from her drawer and and began to twist it between her fingers. "Furthermore, the last child to disappear was Tommy Atkins. He was a big lad for his age, and there were signs of a struggle near where he had been working in the field. This was found at the scene."

Marianne craned her neck to see what it was. "A scrap of material? What possible clue is that?"

Augusta held it up for closer inspection. "A scrap of expensive brocaded silk, with an intricate pattern of stitching. It's from too fancy a piece of clothing for anyone but a fine gentleman to have been wearing."

"It could be a coincidence," answered Marianne, though her voice lacked real conviction. "In any case, it's hardly definitive evidence. I mean, you can hardly begin searching the closets of every gentleman in London for a torn waistcoat."

Augusta's eyes took on a speculative gleam for a moment, then she gave a curt laugh. "I suppose that is out of the question. But nevertheless, it is the only clue I have, so I must begin somewhere." She turned her journal around and pushed it toward her sister. "You are more aware than I of all the gentlemen in our area," she said with a touch of humor. "Am I missing anyone?"

Marianne took several minutes to study the pages. "Lord Jeffries, though he's over seventy if he's a day."

"Then let us rule him out for the moment."

"And the new tenant of Chilton Hall. Baron Stoneleigh, I think, though I've not met him. No one has."

Augusta added his name to the list.

"How many are there?"

Her lips pursed as she added up the entries. "Eleven—no, twelve."

Her sister was tactfully silent.

"I know it is no easy task, but there is nothing to

do for it. I shall begin making some discreet inquiries
into the character of each of our suspects and see what
I turn up."

"Oh dear, you must promise to be extremely careful, Gus. If you are right about what is going on, you
are after a very dangerous man."

"If I am right, it is *he* who had better watch out."

Augusta hardly noticed the break in the music. She
was enjoying a comfortable coze with Baron Ashford,
one of her oldest friends from home and a name she
hadn't bothered to put on her list. He had already
been most helpful, chattering on with only the slightest
urging about several of their neighbors, but she dared
not push too hard. Still, she had decided she could
eliminate two of her suspects, while a third looked to
merit closer scrutiny.

"Forgive me, Gus, but I must excuse myself and
find my next partner. Shall I escort you back to your
mama or your sister?"

"Thank you, Jamie, but I am quite happy to sit here
for a spell."

He bent over her hand. "Can't imagine why you
choose to act like a turbaned matron and refuse to
set foot on the floor."

"You know I prefer not to dance. My bones are
too creaky to climb down from the shelf."

They both smiled. It had become a joke between
them, her unmarried state. He had offered for her
once, at the end of her first Season, though she had
always felt it was more from loyalty than any deeper
emotion. When she had gently but firmly refused, he
had seemed rather relieved. Now he was more like
the older brother she no longer had, and she much
preferred it that way, since she would never have any
more than sisterly feelings for him.

"I shall see you later, then."

He withdrew into the crowd and Augusta took a
moment to survey the room. Marianne was sur-

rounded by a bevy of admirers, but there was no cause for concern. All were perfectly acceptable young men, so she felt free to turn her attention to the crush of people gathered in the soaring space. In the flickering light of the myriad candles, it was difficult to discern whether any of the gentlemen she was interested in were present. Perhaps she could ask Jamie later—

"Miss Hadley." The rise in tone indicated it was not the first time the gentleman had spoken her name.

Her head jerked around.

"I asked if I might be allowed the pleasure of this dance."

She stared at Sheffield in disbelief. "You are asking *me* to dance? Aren't you afraid I might tread on your toes or cause you to trip and split your pantaloons?"

He gave a low chuckle and her insides gave a small lurch. It was the first real smile she had seen on his face, and its effect was rather . . . devastating. "Ah, but this time I shall be on guard against any havoc you might wreak on my person."

She forced her eyes away. "You needn't bother. I never dance."

Ignoring her assertion, he reached for her hand.

"G-go away."

"Come now," he murmured. "I have come to know you are capable of a more scathing setdown than that. Perhaps something that includes 'pompous ass' and 'foul-mouthed popinjay'?"

Why, the man actually had a sense of humor! Her lips twitched in spite of her resolve to ignore him.

Suddenly, before Augusta quite knew how it had happened, she was on her feet, his hand firmly around her elbow.

"Now why does a pompous ass wish to dance with an idiot?" she asked softly as he guided her out onto the crowded floor.

He didn't answer her. The first notes of a lilting melody drifted though the air, along with the faint scent of cut lilac and tuberoses. There was a rustle of silk as ladies turned to their partners, and Augusta realized it was a waltz that was starting. She opened her mouth to demur, but the earl's hand had already come to rest at the small of her back, drawing her close enough that she could feel the heat from his muscular thighs.

"Relax," he murmured close to her ear. "Follow me and we shall manage to navigate these treacherous waters without sinking another couple or running aground on the platter of lobster patties."

That he was an excellent dancer came as no surprise to her, for she had already noticed how he moved with a lithe grace, entirely masculine, that exuded an undercurrent of coiled strength. That she matched his steps without effort was a bit more of a shock. Though accorded to have a natural rhythm herself, she had expected that nerves would deaden her limbs into awkward stiffness. But after the first few halting movements, she forgot all about being self-conscious, letting the music and his subtle touch sweep her along. It was several moments before he spoke again.

"What?" Her eyes flew open in some embarrassment. She hadn't even realized they had been shut.

The corners of his mouth curled upward. "I said, for someone who never dances, you are doing quite well."

"Actually, what you mean is, you are relieved that I haven't capsized you into the fountain, ruining yet another waistcoat."

"Ah, but this one is watered silk." There was a decided twinkle in his blue eyes.

A burble of laughter escaped her lips, then she quickly caught herself and composed her features into a more serious mien. Other ladies might find him irresistible, but she did not intend to be seduced by the Earl of Sheffield's charm. "Now, why was it you forced me out here, sir?" she demanded, a bit sharper than she intended.

"Force? I never force ladies to do anything," he said softly.

"No? Do they simply fall on their knees begging . . ." She broke off in some confusion, not exactly sure what she meant to say, and the color rose to her cheeks. To her vast relief, he merely regarded her intently for a moment, then addressed her original question.

"I feel beholden, as a gentleman, to offer you an apology. Two of them, that is. My language during our past . . . encounters was inexcusable."

She looked up at him. "It was. But I suppose it was greatly provoked. A gentleman of your stature does not take kindly to being knocked on his rump."

It was his turn to laugh, and he made no attempt to stifle the rich baritone sound. "You should know, you have accomplished what no other man, not even Gentleman Jackson, has managed to do."

"Set you down a peg? Someone should do it," she muttered under her breath. "Seeing as you have a high enough opinion of yourself."

He cocked his head to one side. "What was that?"

"Oh, never mind," she said in a louder tone. "You may consider yourself forgiven, though I can't fathom why it makes a whit of difference to you."

His arm suddenly tightened around her waist and he quickened their steps, turning her in a series of intricate figures that left her a little breathless.

"It doesn't," he finally replied. "I care very little for what other people think. However, regardless of what you choose to believe, Miss Hadley, I wish you to know that I regret my earlier rudeness. We seem to have gotten off on the wrong foot with each other, but it appears we are making some strides to reaching a common ground of civility."

He was subtly clever in his choice of words, she had to give him that. It only made her feel more awkward and unpolished. "How is it you know my name?"

"Ah, that is right, we have not been introduced. Not formally." He inclined his head a fraction. "Allow me to correct that. I am Alexander Phelps—"

"I know very well who you are, Lord Sheffield," she muttered, more aware than she wished to be of the pressure of his gloved hand on small of her back, and the faint, woodsy aroma of his cologne.

"Do you?" His smiled was half mocking.

Augusta felt a rush of anger. Was this his intention, to fluster her with his smooth spins of speech so that she became a stammering fool again, at the mercy of his so-called wit? Perhaps he thought it a suitable revenge to embarrass and humiliate her, just as she had done to him, however unwittingly. Well, she refused to be cowed so easily. "Indeed, sir—you are a rake and a wastrel that Society looks up to because of your title and your fortune. As for doing anything good or useful, I doubt you have ever lifted a finger to do aught but satisfy your own selfish desires."

For a moment there was a flicker of some emotion in his eyes, then his face became very stony. The smile remained carved on his lips, but there was no humor in it. "How very perceptive of you, Miss Hadley. Allow me to congratulate you—your knowledge of all things, be they books or people, seems . . . unquestionable."

The rest of the dance proceeded in grim silence. He still moved with faultless precision, but Augusta could feel the rigid tension in his body. She should have felt pleased, she told herself. After all, she could tell she had managed to land a blow to his precious self-image. But somehow she didn't. It hadn't been anger or embarrassment that she had glimpsed in his eyes. It had been pain. For some odd reason, her angry retort had hurt him.

Her brow furrowed as she stared into the folds of his cravat. It didn't make any sense. He had just finished saying he didn't care what anyone thought, so why should her words have the least effect on him? She had imagined a man of his reputation to be lacking in all sensibilities, yet it seemed he was not without a certain vulnerability.

Perhaps she was as guilty as he had been in pronouncing judgment on a stranger.

The last notes died away and the earl escorted her back to her chair. He bowed over her hand with icy politeness, his eyes avoiding any contact with hers. "I shall leave you to enjoy the rest of the evening in more congenial company."

"Sir," she said quietly as he made to walk away.

He raised his brows in question.

"Now it is my turn to say I'm sorry."

His expression remained impassive. "Why, whatever for?"

"What I said was terribly rude."

"No, Miss Hadley. What you said was the truth."

Then he turned on his heel and disappeared into the crowd.

Chapter Three

I hope this clarification serves to answer some of the astute questions you raised concerning my essay on why an advanced society should grant certain rights to women.

To that end, I must admit that although I am not entirely in agreement with your point of view on the subject, your deft wit and keen observation afforded me more than a few smiles.

You say that you wonder why I favor rights for women when, in your experience, females have shown little capacity for rational thought, and still less for original ideas. However true your observations may be, you may be guilty of judging too harshly. Have you considered the restraints we impose on our females, especially those fresh from the schoolroom. Only think of it—anxious mamas hover over them, ready to pounce on the slightest show of natural ebullience or guileless opinion lest it frighten away some eligible suitor. In public, under the watchful eye of spiteful gossips and straightlaced tabbies, one misstep can result in ostracism, while rakes and fortunehunters think it a game to create ruined reputations. Why, it is a wonder girls dare open their mouths at all!

The earl paused for a moment in reading, struck yet again by the insight and sensitivity his newfound correspondent showed. The fellow must have sisters, he mused, to show such compassionate understanding of the problems faced by ladies in Society. He rubbed at his chin. The letter pointed out a whole new perspective he had never considered. Taking another sip of his brandy, he sighed and continued on.

> Now, I cannot argue that young ladies of a certain age cannot be silly indeed. But can we honestly say that young men are any better? Only look at the young cubs freshly arrived in Town who ape the design of a waistcoat or wear shirtpoints so high as to resemble some strange species of avian life, unable to move their heads more than a degree to the left or right. And then there are the silly pranks, most of which a schoolboy would be roundly caned for, but which we dismiss as merely showing spirit. Add to that the excess of drinking, the gambling away of family fortunes, and I daresay we cannot claim that men show a good deal more intelligence than the opposite sex. . . .

Sheffield couldn't restrain a bark of laughter. Why, the fellow had hit the nail on the head. Men were wont to be as ridiculous as females, he admitted. And it was true that they were allowed a good deal more leeway in such silly behavior. Now that he thought about it, a man was allowed to mature from a child into an adult with no real consequences for making the normal mistakes along the way, whereas a lady was accorded no such freedom. One error and she was ruined for life. It *was* deuced unfair! His friend was right—he should try not to judge quite so harshly.

A rueful grimace stole across his lips as the letter and its discussion of females brought to mind his recent confrontations with a certain lady. He had been wrong to think her bird-witted and flighty. She was neither. Nor was she as clumsy as he had supposed at first. In his arms, she had moved with a sinuous silkiness that had both surprised and pleased him. Even now he could recall the sway of her gently rounded hips, the smooth rhythm of her long legs matching his own moves with ease. He had also been all too aware of the shapely swell of her breasts close to his chest, the arch of her neck, the feel of her slender fingers in his.

Damnation. He was growing aroused at the very thought of the maddening chit.

He took another gulp of brandy, reminding himself that it was absurd to dwell on her. It was clear she held him in nothing but contempt. And what did it matter that a rather shrewish young lady listened to gossip and rushed to make her own hasty judgments? There were plenty of ladies far more beautiful who did not look on him with such blazing dislike, who would welcome his attentions with far more than feisty words. Yet he didn't seem quite able to banish those flashing eyes from his thoughts. They hinted at an intensity and depth of spirit which, along with her willowy form and unusual looks, he found strangely compelling.

Or perhaps intriguing was a better word. She was, after all, hardly a typical young miss. When roused to anger, she did not shrink from displaying a quick tongue and firm opinions, as well as the courage to express them, even to gentlemen. After a moment of reflection, he had to add that she was not lacking in more delicate sensibilities either. Not many people would have been perceptive enough to see the subtle change that had come over him. She had sensed that her words had found a chink in his armor of studied indifference, but rather than triumph in her eyes, there had been remorse, as if she had regretted causing him any pain.

His hand threaded through his long locks. He had never been bothered by attacks on his character before, but for some reason, it irked him that Edwin Hadley's sister had such a low opinion of him. Unfortunately, her words were not without merit. Harsh though they may have been, there was more truth to their essence than he cared to admit. He might not be a real cad or a bounder, but he had been essentially a selfish man since his days at university. On that she was right.

He shifted uncomfortably in his chair and reread both letters he had received from Firebrand. His eyes then strayed to the pile of pamphlets and books on his desk. Whether goaded by Miss Hadley's stinging words or inspired by his new friend's bold ideas he wasn't sure, but he began to mull over a plan that had been in the back of head for some time.

Augusta crossed another name off of her list. Marianne had learned from one of her dance partners that Viscount Mansfield had sailed for his family's estate in Barbados over four months ago. Such information, she decided, ruled him out as a likely candidate. Her eyes scanned over the page as she drummed her fingers on the tooled leather blotter.

That left six.

She was well aware that narrowing down the rest was going to be extremely difficult. The information gathered from Baron Ashford and several other old friends from home had allowed her to progress this far, but now inquiries into the character and habits of the remaining suspects became a good deal trickier. A way must be found to delve into their private affairs, but discreetly, so as not to raise any suspicion. It would be much easier, she thought with an exasperated sigh, if she were a man. What she needed to hear were the sorts of things men bandied about over a bottle of port at their clubs.

Marianne had suggested taking Ashford into her confidence, but she had rejected the idea out of hand. Jamie was a stalwart friend, entirely trustworthy and not without a certain intelligence, but his judgment was not as sharp as she might have wished. Bluff and

honest himself, he failed to grasp the need for circum-
spection in certain situations. In this case, an unguarded word at the wrong moment might turn all her
careful plans to naught. Besides, the person she sought
might well prove to be a friend of his, and gentlemen
could have the oddest notions about honor and that
sort of thing. No, he was best left unaware of the
entire matter.

With a sigh, Augusta snapped her journal shut and
locked it in the top drawer. Perhaps she would think
of something later, while trying to ignore the warbling
soprano screeches emitting from the oldest of the six
Dulcett daughters at the upcoming evening musicale
orchestrated by the girl's mother. If Augusta had not
known better, she might have suspected the lady of
possessing a wickedly sly sense of humor to think of
revealing that Miss Dulcett's tones were anything but.
However, it was unlikely there would be any but the
most boring of conversations and music at the gathering.

At least it was not a ball, she thought. She wouldn't
have to worry about being roused from her normal
routine of sitting quietly off to one side, choosing to
let her thoughts and ideas do the lively capering instead of her feet. Though she enjoyed dancing, there
were precious few gentlemen who moved her in any
interesting way.

A faint color rose to her cheeks as she recalled the
firm grip of Sheffield's long fingers, the solid breadth
of his chest, the effortless grace of his steps in swirling
her across the floor. There was no denying that *that*
man moved in interesting ways. That he possessed a
dry sense of humor and a devastating smile was a
more surprising discovery, especially as he had not
been wont to display either in their previous meetings.
More than that, his eyes, when not clouded with anger,
revealed a depth of emotion she wouldn't have
guessed at either. Contrary to her first opinion, the
earl did not appear to be as shallow as she had
thought. He might be selfish, arrogant, and quick to

anger, but he was also witty, charming, and more vulnerable than he cared to admit.

The clock on her mantel chimed to remind her that it was time to start dressing for the evening, but still she sat staring into the flickering logs. Well, it hardly mattered what sort of man he was. Her stinging setdown had made it quite certain that she was not likely to find herself waltzing in his arms again any time soon.

Now why did such a thought leave her feeling far from gratified?

The evening proved to be even worse than she had imagined. The young lady had chosen a difficult aria that only served to highlight her woefully inadequate range. She plunged into the notes with nary a care for the crescendos or adagios of the piece, drawing a pained wince from those who had even a cursory interest in music. Augusta let her eyes fall shut for a moment, wishing such action might block out the sound as well as the sight of the unfortunate girl laboring away beside the piano.

An elbow nudged into her side. "How can you even think of nodding off?" whispered Marianne.

"Rest assured that if I had any such intention, I should soon find myself disabused of the notion. Why, Gideon may dispense with his trumpet and merely take Miss Dulcett along as his companion in order to wake the dead."

Her sister stifled a giggle, drawing a stern look from their mother.

"Do not fidget, child. Men do not like such hoydenish behavior."

"Yes, Mama," murmured Marianne.

Lady Farnum turned her attention to her eldest daughter. "And you Augusta, I should hope you would not encourage her in such unladylike ways," she said with a sniff. "Just because *you* do not choose to make yourself agreeable with—"

A high note cut off the rest of the sentence. It

hardly mattered. Augusta knew it all by heart. Her
mother could not understand what interest books or
ideas held for a female, especially when said female
had not yet attended to the infinitely more important
matter of attaching a suitable husband. She gave an
inward sigh, knowing what a sad disappointment she
had proved to be in the eyes of at least one parent.
Well, her mother need have no such laments concerning her youngest child. Marianne's stunning looks and
sunny disposition had attracted a swarm of eligible
suitors, and she would have only to choose which one
she favored to ensure there would be an engagement
by the end of the Season.

August shifted uncomfortably in her seat, drawing
another glare from Lady Farnum. Her father did not
seem as upset that she chose to spend her time in
the library reading and studying. Nor had Edwin. Her
brother had encouraged her to use her mind, sharing
his books and his tutor's ideas with her. She found
she had to blink back a tear on recalling the countless
hours they had spent discussing Voltaire or the radical
notions of Mr. Jefferson. And it was not as if he was
some dull dog, without a spark of mischief to leaven
his keen intellect. He had possessed a wicked sense
of humor—his comments on the hapless Miss Dulcett
would no doubt have had her drawing even more censure from her mother.

Lord, she missed him.

The singer finally warbled to an end and refresh-
ments were announced. Marianne was immediately
surrounded by several young gentlemen who had
never shown the slightest interest in music before.
Seeing that her mother was already engaged in a comfortable coze with a few of her old friends, including
the formidable Lady Sefton, Augusta rose to mingle
with the rest of the guests. She took up a glass of
lemonade and drifted toward the french doors leading
to the garden, her brow furrowing as she pondered
how to turn the evening to some use in continuing her

investigation. There were very few people here she knew past a nodding acquaintance, and certainly none with whom she could have any plausible reason to bring up mention of the six gentlemen she wished to know more about.

"I suggest you pay attention to your surroundings while handling such a lethal substance," came a low voice from over her shoulder.

The result, naturally, was that several drops sloshed over the hem of her gown. She did not need to turn around to identify the speaker. To her chagrin, she felt her cheeks begin to turn a dull red.

"Your waistcoat may count itself avenged, sir."

"I should like to inform it of the fact, but alas, it has suffered an early demise due the injuries sustained during your unprovoked attack."

"Hardly unprovoked," she countered, trying hard not to show her amusement. The man did have the dry sort of humor that she appreciated best. It reminded her of . . . She forced such thoughts aside and her eyes strayed down to the small stain. "That was not well done of you, sir."

"Ah, but then you already know I am sadly lacking in character." His hand came around her elbow and propelled her through the open doors. "You look as though you could use a breath of fresh air." He slanted a sideways look her face. "A trifle warm inside?"

"No, I find that music always transports me to great emotion," she said through gritted teeth.

He chuckled. "Yes, like the impulse to do bodily harm—this time on a more vocal object than a waistcoat."

Augusta turned to study a bower of climbing roses in order to hide her grudging smile. "I doubt you have brought me out on the terrace to discuss murder—either that of a cherished item of your wardrobe or that of the daughter of our host."

Sheffield took a step closer. "Well, you have to admit that she deserves to be throttled."

Why was it that the heat in her cheeks was refusing to fade, she wondered? In fact, his physical presence was making her a bit warm all over. "She is not well endowed with talent, I grant you."

"None whatsoever," he replied. "However, the chit is well endowed in other ways."

Augusta hoped her face was not as burning as it felt. "Your credentials as a music critic may be suspect, but you are obviously an expert on *that* sort of thing," she said with some asperity. "Now kindly step aside and allow me to return inside. And please cease attempting to humiliate me for whatever wrongs you feel you have suffered. I have told you, I am sorry for slaying your waistcoat and sorry for my sharp words of the other night, but somehow I doubt the wound to your pride will prove mortal."

Sheffield didn't move. "You think I am trying to humiliate you?"

"Why else would you seek me out? I am hardly . . . endowed with any of the attributes that would attract a man such as yourself. As you yourself said, I am clumsy, old, and ill-tempered." She paused a fraction. "And the bodice of my gown does not threaten to split its seams every time I take a breath."

The earl regarded the swell of her breasts. "No, but there appears to be nothing to criticize on that account," he murmured.

"Insufferable lout," she said under her breath as she tried to push past him.

His hand once again was on her elbow, his head close to her ear. "Come now, Miss Hadley, did your brother never tease you?"

She froze. Then without warning her hand came hard across his cheek. "How dare you speak of my brother, you indolent wastrel. He was worth a hundred of your sort—" To her mortification, her voice broke and several tears spilled from her eyes. Her mother's earlier carping, the mounting frustration over how to further her investigation, and the sudden pang of longing for her older sibling had rubbed her nerves raw, making the earl's playful banter feel like a knife cutting across an open wound. "Oh . . . damnation," she muttered, brushing roughly at her cheeks with the sleeve of her gown.

Ignoring the red welt spreading across his face, Sheffield took a heavy silk handkerchief from his pocket and handed it to her without a word. There were a few moments of awkward silence before he finally spoke. "I imagine you miss him terribly," he said softly.

Augusta nodded and steadied herself with a deep breath. "He was the very best of men," she said simply. "He was wise, funny, and kind. He encouraged me to pursue what interested me, no matter what anyone else thought, and he was always there whenever I needed advice." She broke off and turned to stare out at the darkened garden, arms folded tightly across her chest. Even to Marianne she had never admitted the depth of her sense of loss, yet here she had just blurted out her most private feelings to a man she did not even like, much less esteem. Her jaw set in embarrassment and anger at letting his words cause her to reveal so vulnerable a part of herself. The earl must be smugly satisfied to have discovered that she was naught but another silly female, and one prone to turning into a watering pot at that.

Her shoulders hunched, waiting for the inevitable sarcastic reply.

"It is entirely understandable that you feel his loss so keenly," he said quietly. "Edwin was indeed all that was good. One could not ask for a more loyal or compassionate friend. His quick thinking extricated my younger brother from a youthful indiscretion that could have had dire consequences, and for that alone I shall always be grateful." He cleared his throat. "I wrote to your father on hearing of his death, but when

I learned you were his sister, I wished to express my condolences to you as well for your loss." There was another slight pause. "That, Miss Hadley, is the reason why I have sought out your presence, not for any other purpose."

Augusta stared at him in mute surprise.

"Though you may find it hard to believe, your brother and I considered each other friends," he continued. "We enjoyed each other's company—"

"I can't imagine why. Edwin did not drink to excess or risk his fortune on a turn of the cards or seduce other men's wives," she snapped, covering her shock and confusion over his unexpected revelation by lashing out at him again.

His lips compressed. "For one who is wont to rake another person over the coals for passing hasty judgments, you are remarkably stubborn in clinging to your own prejudices. But since that is evidently the case, I shall endeavor not to inflict my unworthy company on you again, as it is obviously distasteful to you."

Color flamed in Augusta's face, this time from shame, not anger.

"However," he added stiffly, "if you ever find yourself in need of the sort of advice you would ask of your brother, you may always feel free to come to me."

"I cannot imagine that ever happening, sir," she replied haltingly, keeping her eyes averted from his. "Nonetheless, I . . . thank you. It is a most generous offer."

"Augusta?" Marianne's slender form was silhouetted against the brightly lit room. Along with that of one of her many admirers. "Do you wish to join Mr. Collingworth and me for supper? Jamie has arrived as well."

"Yes, I shall be happy to come," she answered. Her fingers fumbled awkwardly with the white silk square before thrusting it back into the earl's hand. "I had best go in." She drew in a ragged breath. "I am sorry.

We simply don't seem to rub together well." The corners of her mouth came up in an attempt at a smile. "Nothing but sparks between us, I'm afraid. So perhaps it is for the better that we avoid each other's presence."

Sheffield's expression was inscrutable as he inclined his head a fraction. "As you wish, Miss Hadley."

She looked as if to speak again, then merely swallowed hard before turning and walking quickly back inside.

It was some time later before the earl left off standing on the stone terrace and made an early departure from the festivities.

Augusta's spirits ebbed even lower as she watched the earl take his leave. On reflection, she couldn't help but feel her behavior had been nothing short of shameful. His overture of sympathy had been—quite literally—thrown back in his face. She cringed at the very thought of what she had done. No matter what his faults or peccadillos, he had not deserved such shabby treatment at her hands.

She bit her lip, wondering what had come over her of late. It was not like her to be so unfair. Though she tried to tell herself that the earl had shown himself to be arrogant, rude, and puffed up with a sense of his own importance, she had to admit that he was also humorous, clever, and thoughtful. How many men would have taken such a slap and vile insult without falling into a paroxysm of outrage? Yet he had simply handed her his handkerchief, followed by more comforting words, as if he had somehow understood that her actions had more to do with her own wrenching grief than anything he had said or done.

And what had she done but strike out again, hurling yet more unwarranted aspersion on his character? She swallowed hard, wishing she could rid herself of the sour taste in her mouth. He had been right—she was as guilty as the worst gossips and tattlemongers of the *ton,* basing her judgment of him on sketchy rumor and hearsay, then refusing to see any of the subtle hues beneath the bold strokes of black on white. All the things she had heard might be true, but did they really paint a true picture of the man? Her lips pursed. It wasn't likely she would ever know, since she doubted she would ever exchange a private word with him again.

But what she did know was that she had never felt more disappointed in herself—

"Gus," whispered Marianne rather loudly. Her tone indicated it was not merely the second repetition.

Augusta's eyes jerked up from her plate of untouched lobster patties.

"Mr. Collingworth was asking whether you had read the latest offering from the Minerva Press."

"I'm sorry. I'm afraid I was woolgathering." She forced her attention back to the lively conversation taking place, ignoring the pinch of concern on her sister's face.

It was with great relief that Augusta heard her mother's announcement a short while later that she was tired and wished to return home instead of taking up a seat at the whist tables. The carriage was ordered and the wheels had barely started rolling over the cobblestones before a rhythm of bubbly snores, well lubricated by several glasses of champagne, indicated that Lady Farnum had fallen asleep.

Marianne regarded the rigid set of Augusta's jaw in the flickering light. "What's wrong, Gus?"

Augusta shifted against the squabs so that her face was nearly hidden in the shadows.

"You were out on the terrace with Lord Sheffield for rather a long time," ventured her sister. "People were beginning to remark on it. He did not . . . do anything to upset you, did he? I cannot imagine that even he would be so reckless as to—"

"There was nothing untoward about Lord Sheffield's behavior," she said tightly. After a moment she added, "It is my own that is deserving of censure."

Marianne looked puzzled. "Whatever can you mean?"

Augusta hesitated. How could she begin to explain her feelings? Her sister sailed through life, content to deal with the swirls and eddys on the surface waters without ever delving into the murky depths below. It was not to say Marianne was shallow—far from it— just that she preferred to turn her cheeks to the sun, steering away from all hint of storm. Augusta found it much more difficult to navigate such a smooth course. Somehow she was always falling overboard into the waves and chop.

A sigh escaped her lips. There was much she could share with her sister, but there was also much that was best left unsaid.

"It's not important," she finally answered. "The two of us simply do not get along, and I'm afraid I was frightfully rude again—though this time the lemonade ended up on me rather than him."

Marianne still appeared perturbed. "I don't understand. The two of you don't even know each other— what could you possibly be quarreling about?"

Augusta winced inwardly at the unintentional jab. "As I said, nothing of import. And it won't happen again. We have agreed it is best to stay out of each other's path, so that's an end to it." The way she turned to stare out of the small-paned window made it clear that she also wished the conversation to be at an end.

Her sister took the hint and lapsed into her own private thoughts.

Augusta kept her eyes on the vague shapes and shadows that were ghosting past. Sometimes her emotions were as hard to decipher, she mused, and as quixotic as the mist swirling up from the river. It was strange how one moment everything could seem sharp and clear, only to dissolve from view in the next instant.

She longed to voice such thoughts to someone who might understand what she meant.

Edwin would have understood. But now? Her mouth quirked in a odd little smile. Why, the only person she knew who might catch the drift of her re- flections was the anonymous *Tinder*. His last few let- ters had revealed a man—she was sure it was a man— of surprising sensitivity as well as sharp intellect. He had even set down on paper a few personal musings of his own.

Her expression softened. The hints at weariness and opportunities wasted that he had let drop led her to believe he must be quite advanced in years. It was a shame, for she had certainly encountered no other gentlemen who sparked even the slightest interest for her, while he . . . he intrigued her.

Then she forced a harsh laugh at herself. What a notion! It was just like her, to fashion a pen-and-paper romance in her head because she was incapable of hav- ing one with a flesh-and-blood gentleman. The fellow was probably eighty and squinted. She gave another in- ward laugh. It wasn't as if she were contemplating getting legshackled to the gentleman, merely sharing some of her private thoughts. He had been willing to bare a part of himself. Perhaps she should consider doing the same. It would be such a help to be able to voice her doubts and fears to someone else. What pos- sible harm was there in that? After all, she never meant to reveal her true identity.

Chapter Four

. . . *And now that we have come to as close an agreement as we are ever likely to achieve on the matter, I shall turn my pen to some of the more personal issues that your last letter raised. Be assured, my friend, that I am both honored and pleased that you feel you may unburden yourself of some of your most private hopes and fears without fear of censure or ridicule. I think I have come to know you well enough these past few weeks to understand the certain restlessness of spirit beneath your keen intellect. Perhaps it is because those of us who question the nature of things around us are dismayed at finding there are few absolute answers. But I urge you not to become disheartened by the enormity of what you cannot affect. It grieves me to read your admission that sometimes the morning seems too bleak to bother rising for, that you feel too keenly all the ills in the world, including yourself. I know that is not so! You have a sharp mind and more of a sense of right and wrong than you care to admit. Instead of feeling angry at yourself for lost opportunity, find something that heats your blood, and I daresay you will discover it is boredom, not lack of ability, that has you feeling blue-deviled.*

You should know that you are not alone in your thoughts. I, too, find myself confused at times, unable to sift through the chaff of my own

*doubts and fears to find the kernels of real sub-
stance. Why, just the other evening, as I was re-
turning home from a certain festivity . . ."*

Sheffield poured himself another brandy and returned to his comfortable leather chair by the fire.
Light winked off the facets of the cut-crystal glass like
the bright sparks from the crackling logs. His spirits
felt equally ignited. He had been right to trust his
instincts and confide in his anonymous friend. It was
truly amazing what a few wise words of encouragement from a kindred spirit could do.

His eyes strayed to the sheaf of papers spread over
his desk. He now had the courage to put the finishing
touches on what he had been working on for the past
two weeks. It had been a strange sensation at first,
devoting his energy to books and pamphlets rather
than the mindless amusements he was used to. But
now the idea of spending an evening in the heady
company of philosophers and reformers instead of his
usual cronies—whose idea of a thought-provoking discussion would be debating whether a good claret was
preferable to champagne—had become as intoxicating
as the copious amounts of spirits he had been in the
habit of imbibing.

A wry smile pulled at his lips. No doubt most of
his friends would think him dicked in the nob for
what he was about to embark on. Not that he cared.
He found he had truly become interested in the plight
of children forced into labor, especially in the coal
mines in the north. Sparked by Firebrand's first essay,
he had sought to learn more, and what he had discovered had shocked and then outraged him. How could
a civilized society tolerate such abuses, he wondered,
though he knew full well the answer. The people who
could effect a change—people like himself—preferred
to remain blind to such ills. And they would hardly
thank him for seeking to open their eyes, of that he
had little illusion.

While that mattered very little, he did find himself wondering what his newfound friend would think. He was almost tempted to reveal his plan, even though that would mean giving away his true identity, for he wished the fellow's frank opinion of his actions. Actually, if truth be told, he wished his friend's approval, and even admiration. Like many of the feelings he had been experiencing lately, that was a novel one as well. Approval and admiration had always rained down upon him so easily that he had never consciously sought them. Yet they had come for all the wrong reasons. Now, for once, he wished to be truly deserving of such sentiments.

The amber spirits spun in a slow vortex as Sheffield swirled his glass before the light. The look of bemusement on his lean features only deepened on thinking more of the budding friendship that was beginning to take root between the two correspondents. Not only had Firebrand given him encouragement, but the fellow had also begun to share his own doubts and fears. It seemed both of them had developed enough of a trust to reveal their most intimate feelings. With a start, he realized how much the rather odd relationship had come to mean to him.

And yet it was ironic, really. They were probably acquainted with each other, and had even conversed on occasion at one of the frivolous entertainments they no doubt both attended. His friend claimed that only family obligations forced him to go out, and even then, he avoided most conversation and remained aloof from the usual inanities. But they were sure to have met at some point. Why, his new friend could be Heppleworth, the gouty old baron who hobbled about with the aid of a silver-tipped walking stick, or Symington, the quiet gentleman from the north who was said to collect bats and beetles.

Indeed, it could be anyone!

He shook his head. It was doubtful he was the only one who took care to disguise his true views behind

the mask of rigid manners and studied indifference
that the *ton* all but demanded of its members. No
wonder that Society seemed so shallow. After a sip or
two, the earl found himself moved to put down his
glass and take up his pen to put such thoughts to
paper.

The next morning, he rose early and spent the
morning in his library, putting the finishing touches on
his work, all the while fighting down a fluttering of
nervous anticipation, as if he were a callow schoolboy
about to embrace a woman for the first time. His carriage was brought around. He took one last look in
the mirror to straighten the already perfect folds of
his cravat and brush the imaginary wrinkles from his
coat, then took up his hat and a slim moroccan leather
portfolio and descended the marble steps of his
townhouse.

It proved not quite so difficult as he imagined.
Though he found his mouth dry as cotton and his
throat so constricted that it seemed no words could
possibly squeeze out, he managed to rasp out a hesi-
tant beginning. As confidence took wing, his voice
steadied and rose, his sentences soaring through the
vaulted chamber. The faces before him betrayed a
gamut of emotions, from total shock, to wary specula-
tion, to outright amusement. When he was done, a
smattering of applause was overwhelmed by simple
silence. No one was quite sure how to interpret the
true meaning of his carefully chosen words. He could
hardly blame them if they were all wondering what
the deuce the Earl of Sheffield was about, giving a
speech in the House of Lords. No doubt they found
the notion a bit absurd, but perhaps that would soon
change.

"I say, Sheff, tell me what blunt you managed to wrest
out of Copley's pocket by pulling such a stunt!" cried
Lord Dunham as the earl handed his walking stick
and hat to the porter at White's. "By God, I nearly

wept with laughter at hearing of it. Wish you'd let me place a wager of my own, for no matter how daunting the challenge, I know you always find a way to win in the end."

"Aye," chimed in another of his friends. "Always knew you were the cleverest of us all, but how even you managed to pull off such a feat has me in awe." He raised a glass in salute. "I vow, 'tis the best joke yet this Season."

A chorus of laughter rang out, followed by more friendly gibes. "Whoever did you find to write the bloody speech? Haddington says it actually made some sort of sense—that is, if you are some prosy bore with radical ideas."

Sheffield walked slowly to a chair near the crackling fire and sat down, Motioning for a newspaper to be brought over, he opened its ironed pages with a decided snap. "It was no joke," he answered from behind the printed paper.

A few more chuckles sounded, though this time they sounded more tentative.

"Oh come now, Sheff, you've no need to play a charade any longer," said Dunham, a broad grin stretched out across his pudgy face. He gave a conspiratorial wink. "Tell us who you have roasted so we may go stick a fork in him."

The earl lowered the newsprint. "Perhaps I've become a prosy bore with radical ideas."

The smiles faded, replaced by expressions of uncertainty.

"You can't be serious!" exclaimed Viscount Grenwald. "You have too much sense to . . . to become a sensible fellow on us, Sheff."

"Come to think of it, he ain't been around much these past few weeks," groused Dunham. "The devil take it, next thing you'll tell us is you're contemplating getting legshackled."

There were groans all around.

"I've not sunk quite that far into lunacy," replied the earl dryly.

Grenwald shook his head mournfully. "Far enough, though. I was about to propose a toast, but perhaps it had better be a eulogy to the hearty fellow we once knew."

"I'm hardly dead, Fitz, more like I've just woken up to certain things."

His friends looked at him with something akin to bewilderment. "Dash it all, I need a glass of claret to help swallow all this," grumbled Dunham. The others quickly voiced their agreement. "Coming, Sheff?" he added as they all got to their feet.

"I'll join you in a bit, as soon as I finish this article."

Dunham turned away, muttering darkly under his breath.

As the small group quitted the room, another man rose from one of the oversized wingchairs by the fire. "You would do well to heed the advice of your friends, Sheffield. It's rather foolish of a man to get involved in things he knows nothing about," he said in a light voice.

The earl cocked one dark eyebrow. "You are entirely right. So you may rest assured that I mean to learn as much as I can about the subject."

The other man looked taken aback. "Whatever for? What possible interest can it be to you?" His eyes narrowed ever so slightly. "After all, one would hardly think of you as possessing the . . . temperament or the inclination for such causes. I can't fathom why you should risk making a cake of yourself in public."

"I'm touched by your concern for my reputation," replied Sheffield coolly. "But if I choose to make a fool of myself, that is my concern."

The gentleman shrugged and made a show of brushing a mote of dust from the sleeve of his immaculate burgundy swallow-tailed coat. "I merely wished to offer some friendly advice. You know what they say—a little knowledge can be a dangerous thing." The casual smile still on his face, he took his leave of the earl and continued on his way out.

"But if you choose to begin nosing around where you shouldn't," he added to himself, "that is *my* concern."

Augusta put down the newspaper with an unladylike snort. It was outside enough that the earl had unsettled her private thoughts. Now he was playing some sort of May Game with the cause closest to her heart. Confound the man! She almost wished she would run into him again so that she could tell him what she thought of such behavior. Her lips compressed—no, on second thought, she wouldn't be able to say a thing, not without revealing a passion that was best kept hidden away. Once again she muttered an inward curse at the constraints on females. It was most annoying to have to keep her opinions stifled in all but one forum. But at least her ire at the earl had inspired the topic for her next essay.

The time seemed right for a ringing peal at the indifferent attitude of the privileged class, who chose to turn a blind eye on the misfortunes of those beneath them. Sheffield's speech, though no doubt inspired by some practical joke, contained a number of sensible ideas, even though she was loath to admit it. He had hinted that the *ton* must shoulder some of the blame for allowing such horrors to exist. She would elaborate on the theme, even though Pritchard was becoming a tad nervous over the increasing heat of her tone. But he'd not kick up a dust quite yet, not while people still flocked to buy his publication to see what the latest incendiary words from Firebrand would be.

However, the essay could wait for later. She put aside the paper to regard the thick sheets of cream stationery that lay folded on her desk. It was strange how her pulse quickened when the envelope, addressed in the bold, sweeping stroke she had come to recognize immediately, appeared on the butler's silver tray. She found she looked forward to the arrival of her friend's letters—for friend was how she thought of him. Considering the intimacies they had exchanged, they could be no less.

She repressed a slight smile on recalling some of the words on the pages before her. As he himself had said, it appeared that both of them had become unfashionably honest with each other, laying bare their most private emotions, which they dared not to reveal to anyone else. The smile stole back as she reread his half-joking suggestion that they meet at White's to share a bottle of port and conversation long into the night. So he, too, felt the writing of letters was becoming increasingly frustrating, what with the ideas that always seemed woefully unexplored, the questions that remained unanswered until the next missive arrived. However, if he only knew how impossible his wish was, and not for the reasons he imagined!

She took up her pen to finish off her reply.

> . . . . *As to your sentiments that an evening at one of our clubs would prove most delightful, I have no doubt that would in many ways be true. But think on it. Part of the honesty we have derives, no doubt, from the anonymity. Much as I should enjoy meeting you face to face and pursuing our talks in a much more animated way, I fear that it might mean risking a friendship that has become quite special, at least to me, or altering it in ways that neither of us would care to do. Therefore, I think it best to continue as we have. . . .*

A final paragraph followed, then the letter was set aside for the afternoon post. Augusta turned her attention to more mundane things—penning several replies to invitations, copying out a recipe for chilblains for Lady Setterwhite, sending off a report of what she had learned so far to Mrs. Roberts at Greenfield

Manor—before her thoughts came back to pages meant for her friend. She chewed thoughtfully on the end of her pen. It was clear from numerous asides he had let drop that he moved in the highest circles. Also more than apparent was the fact that he possessed a sharp mind and a keen eye for observation. Her lips pursed, then she reached for the last sheet of her letter and added an impulsive postscript.

> *Perhaps I should not be so bold as to ask, but there is a matter on which I could use your help. . . .*

The last chords of a lively country dance ended with a flourish, leaving the capering couples flushed with a touch of color. Augusta watched Marianne laugh merrily at some whispered remark from her partner, which elicited not only a besotted smile from the favored fellow but a collective sigh from the group of young gentlemen awaiting her return from the dance floor. With such unaffected charm, angelic blonde looks, and sweet disposition, her sister seemed to inspire a rapturous response from even a number of the jaded bucks. Her hand was quickly claimed for the next set, and already the fellow was staring at her like a bewitched mooncalf.

Augusta's fingers began to trace the subtle pattern of the new brocaded silk gown Marianne had chosen for her as she wondered for a flitting moment what it would be like to inspire such passionate emotion in a gentleman. It was a silly thought, she knew, and one hardly likely to come to pass. Even a handsome dowry and influential family could not overcome the aversion men felt toward an outspoken, opinionated female whose beanpole figure and angular face only accentuated how little she resembled the ideal sort of wife. In another moment, her wistful expression changed to one of detached amusement on considering that the only little frisson she was likely to inspire in a member of the opposite sex would be one of immense relief at not having to face a life legshackled to an aging antidote.

At least her words, however anonymous, seemed capable of stirring the souls of some people. She would have to be satisfied with that.

"You appear to be contemplating some private joke." Baron Ashford took a seat beside her. "Care to share it?"

"Hmmmm." Augusta pushed her reveries aside. "I doubt you would appreciate the irony of it." On regarding her friend's slightly injured look, she quickly changed the subject. "Who is that dancing with Marianne?"

Never one to stay miffed for long, Ashford abandoned his pout and swept his gaze over the crush on the dance floor. "Oh, that's Ludlowe," he replied after a bit. "Heir to Cranehill's earldom unless the old stallion can produce an heir with his new bride."

"I didn't realize centaurs were allowed to succeed to the title," she murmured dryly. "What next? Gryphons when some old lion takes to wife a harpy?"

Ashford laughed loud enough to attract the basilisk stare of several turbaned matrons sitting close by. "You are still by far the most interesting lady to talk with, Gus. I shall miss it greatly when . . ." He stopped in some embarrassment.

"When you take a wife?"

His ears turned rather red.

"Well, no doubt there will be other rewards," she murmured, causing his color to deepen to a vivid scarlet. As he struggled to recover his composure, she eyed him thoughtfully. "Who is the lucky lady?"

"Er, well." Ashford tugged at the collar of his shirt, then lowered his voice to a near whisper. "Miss Denton does not seem adverse to my attentions and though I've not spoken as yet . . ." His words trailed off as he watched the lady in question turn a graceful figure in the current set. "Is she not a veritable angel?" he exclaimed in a hushed tone suitable for church.

"An angel," repeated Augusta, with a tad less reverence. "I wish you luck in ascending to heaven, Jamie. Truly I do." On watching the diminutive blonde lower her heart-shaped face and bat her eyelashes at her current partner, she had a feeling her friend was going to need it.

"Then you aren't . . . upset?" ventured Ashford.

"Don't be a gudgeon, Jamie. I have told you, we are much better suited as friends."

He breathed a sigh of relief. "Come, you *must* promise me the next dance, so that I may tell you all about Cynthia."

She did not have the heart to tell him that even a close friendship had its limits, and so, with some reluctance, she allowed herself to be led out.

It was a waltz. The bows of the violins fairly danced over the strings, the notes from the piano lilted to a crescendo, but somehow, her own pulse did not quicken in the quite same way as when she had previously matched her steps to the melody. Ashford's enthusiastic ramblings required little response, giving her a chance to think on what she had just heard.

Ludlowe. It was one of the six names still on her list. She searched her memory to recall what she knew of him, then finally remembered he was the gentleman who had rented the old Trilling estate last Michaelmas quarter. Few in the neighborhood were actually acquainted with him, as he seemed rarely to visit the place.

She glanced toward her sister, who was still in conversation with him as she sat out the waltz. Though his back was to her, Augusta could see he was above average in height, with a fitted coat of hunter-green superfine and fawn pantaloons that bespoke the sure hand of Weston. He wore the clothes well, showing shoulders that needed no wadding or buckram to exaggerate their breadth and strong muscular legs that were no doubt the envy of his less athletic friends. His auburn hair was cut short and artfully arranged in the latest style, and when he turned to bow over her sister's hand, she caught a glimpse of a profile that might have been sculpted by the creators of Lord Elgin's marbles.

"Are you acquainted with Ludlowe, Jamie?" she asked as her friend's flood of praise finally showed signs of ebbing.

It took him a moment to abandon the subject dear to his heart. "Oh, er, not really. Spends most of his time in Town and runs with a a bit different crowd then I am used to."

Augusta darted another quick look at the gentleman in question. "What do you mean?"

He shrugged. "Oh, you know I much prefer the quiet life of the country. Ludlowe is said to enjoy the pleasure of Town. Word is, he's a bang-up horseman, extraordinarily lucky at cards, and a convivial host, which no doubt he can well afford to be, considering his expectations. What makes you ask?"

"No real reason," she snapped, unable to hide the pinch of irritation in her voice. Her present mode of investigating was unearthing precious little information of use. She was going to have to resort to some other method, and soon!

Ashford's brow wrinkled in consternation. "Why—" he began, then his own gaze fell on the conversing couple. "Oh, I see. Is the fellow paying particular attention to Marianne, then?"

"No more than half the eligible bachelors in Town, along with a good deal of unsuitable ones as well," she remarked dryly.

Ashford grinned. "Perhaps the Goddess of Greenfield has a new acolyte kneeling at the altar of her beauty."

"Pray, don't let her hear you repeat that moniker lest you wish her to toss a vase filled with her latest offerings at you."

"And well I know how good her aim is! My head has been hit with far too many apples to make light of such a threat, and so I shall keep a close guard on my tongue in The Incomparable's presence." His expression became more thoughtful. "I hadn't heard that Ludlowe was dangling for a wife, but mayhap he is beginning to think of settling down. Come to think of it, I've not seen him pay the least attention to, er, young misses before, but after all, he is well over thirty and must consider the future."

"I should think Marianne would be happier with someone closer to her own age," she mused. "Rather than with an older man who is likely very set in his ways."

"He's hardly in his dotage, and his family and fortune are more than acceptable. In fact, from what I gather, the fellow would be considered quite a prize on the Marriage Mart."

"Hmmm," was all that Augusta said in reply, but the set of her chin made it clear she was not entirely convinced.

Ashford executed one last spin, nearly treading on both her feet in the process. It took a moment to untangle their steps, and by that time, the music had stopped. "Sorry," he murmured, leading her off to one side of the room. "I have never gotten the knack of that cursed dance. Much too complicated for a fellow to remember all the moves."

Funny, thought Augusta, it hadn't seemed terribly difficult for her partner the last time around.

"Care for a lemonade?" he asked, as he stopped near the set of open french doors leading out to the terraced garden.

"I daresay you have no idea what sort of damage that could lead to. It would be much safer were you to offer plain water. That, at least, leaves no lasting trace."

Augusta's shoulders stiffened at the sound of the baritone voice behind them and to her chagrin, the color began to rise to her cheeks. Ashford looked at her, a question on his lips.

"That is most unfair of you, sir, to call attention to a past . . . accident for which you were at least partly to blame."

"I am beginning to think it was no accident," murmured Sheffield, a note of humor still in his voice. His eyes slowly swept over her new gown, taking in the stylishly low cut of the bodice, the snug capped sleeves, and the way the lush silk clung to the sinewy curves of her form. "You are looking . . . very well this evening, Miss Hadley."

"For a shrewish spinster," she replied through gritted teeth.

The earl's lips repressed a twitch. "Most especially for a shrewish spinster."

Ashford was moved to take another look himself, and his eyes widened slightly. "I say, Gus, you *do* look different." He swallowed hard. "That gown is a vast improvement over your others. You look . . . well, you look . . . very well," he finished lamely, his face now nearly as red as hers. The sound of the musicians warming up for the upcoming country dances spared him any further embarrassment. "Lord, I'm promised to Miss Denton for this next set! You'll excuse me if I take my leave, Gus?" Though worded as a question, he didn't wait to hear the reply. With a cursory nod to Sheffield, he turned and bolted off.

Augusta repressed the desire to aid his progress through the crowd with a well placed kick at his backside. How could he leave her alone in the company of the earl!

As if he could read her thoughts, Sheffield allowed himself a ghost of a smile. "A dull dog indeed," he murmured. His gloved hand came around her elbow and guided her to a quieter spot.

Though feeling in no great charity with her friend at the moment, she felt compelled to come to his defense. "I have no idea what you mean," she said halt-ingly. "Jamie is a solid, intelligent gentleman, and a loyal friend who—"

"Who appears to be blind as a mole, not to speak of his abandoning you for the charms of some un-doubtedly flighty young miss."

"We have been friends since childhood." she said stiffly. "He hardly thinks of me in any other sort of way."

"As I said, a fellow of little imagination." He sig-naled for a nearby footman to approach and took two glasses of champagne from the man's silver tray.

"I was thinking more of ratafia punch, or perhaps a nice claret," she muttered, eyeing the subtle cream-on-cream stripe of his silk waistcoat as he pressed a glass into her hand.

Sheffield gave a deep chuckle. "What? Plans to as-sassinate more than my character?" He took a sip of his drink. "You truly dislike me, don't you?"

Her face was turned toward the darkened garden, obscuring her features. It was several moments before she answered him. "As I have said before, sir, it sim-ply seems that we do not rub together well."

"Hmmm." He regarded her over the rim of his glass, swirling the tiny bubbles to even greater effer-vescence. Augusta suddenly felt his presence doing the same thing to her insides. "I should have thought that one who purports to read Voltaire and Descartes would rely on empirical knowledge, not mere rumor, to pass judgment," he continued in a low voice.

"Ah, but then you don't really believe that a mere female can comprehend such things anyway," she shot back.

"I am relying on my own extensive observations to come to such conclusions," he replied rather dryly.

"It is no wonder, with the sort of female company you obviously keep. In fact, I am amazed that you tolerate any contact with us peabrains at all!"

His eyes drifted down the front of her new gown, which exposed a good deal more flesh than she was used to showing. "Miss Hadley, there are reasons others than discussing philosophy to have, as you say, contact with the opposite sex."

Well aware that her creamy expanse of bosom and bare arms was turning a decided shade of pink, Augusta forgot all her previous charitable thoughts about the earl and was goaded to further heated words. "And no doubt you are well versed in all of them! You should stick to such frivolous pursuits rather than trying to fool people into thinking you give a fig for serious matters. What sort of wager did it take to prompt you to stand up in Parliament and make a mockery of the plight of working children?"

It was the earl's turn to feel stung. "Why do you think it impossible for me have an interest in anything meaningful?"

"For the same reason you think it impossible that *I* can."

That took him aback for a moment. "Well, have you read the books I saw in your arms at Hatchard's?"

"Yes! Would you care to quiz me on them—or perhaps you have not actually looked at them yourself?"

He drew in a sharp breath, then let it out with a reluctant smile. "You are a real firebrand, aren't you," he murmured.

Her eyes grew wide with shock. Ducking her head, she smoothed at the skirt of her gown with slightly trembling fingers. "There seems to be little point in continuing this conversation. Good evening, Lord Sheffield." With that, she walked away as quickly as she dared.

A short while later, safely seated next to several of her mother's close friends, Augusta found that she was still shaking from her confrontation with the earl. What was it about the dratted man that made her forget all her resolutions to keep a rein on her tongue?

Her hands tightened in her lap on recalling his last words.

It was pure coincidence, but she must be more careful in voicing her views, else one of these days she would land herself in real trouble.

Chapter Five

*. . . . It is most unsettling to see a jaded buck of
the* ton *such as the Earl of Sheffield make sport
with a cause that both of us take so seriously.
No doubt it is some mere whim or wager, something akin to betting on which fly shall land in
the claret or which raindrop shall reach the bottom of the pane first, that has set his attention in
that direction, and in another week or so we will
find that he has tired of it and moved on to something else. I should like to know, however, who
drafted his speech, for there were many sensible
observations contained within it. Now, if only
there were truly a gentleman of his stature who
felt as we do, and was willing to stand up and
speak out in good faith. . . ."*

The earl finished reading, then laid aside the latest
letter with a snort of frustration. "The Devil take
it," he muttered under his breath. Had he really such
a rackety reputation that everyone—from an ill-man-
nered chit to a venerable scholar like his friend here—
thought him incapable of aught but frivolous thought?
His hand came up to loosen the carefully knotted cravat at his throat. The damnable thing suddenly felt as
constricting as his own former habits. He yanked it
off with another oath, this one a trifle louder than
before. The fact that a person holding a such low opinion of him was not entirely unjustified was still rather
hard to swallow, but what bothered him most was

what one certain individual thought. His mouth pursed in irritation, for he wanted Firebrand to respect him in person as well as on paper.

To hell with what Edwin Hadley's sister thought.

Well, his own private concerns could wait for later. Right now, he was determined to be of whatever help he could to his friend. He reached for a sheaf of scribbled notes and leafed through them slowly. It had taken over a week, using every resource—reputable and otherwise—to gather such a wealth of interesting information on the six men mentioned in his friend's letter. Why, he never would have guessed that the staid Beckenham would have a stout mistress tucked away in a little cottage in Chiswick, along with a brood of three born on the wrong side of the blanket. Or that the hulking Kendall, who could flatten most any man who stepped into the ring at Gentleman Jackson's, raised delicate orchids.

Both of them had been eliminated in his mind as being capable of any sort of nefarious deed, along with Biddlesworth, who seemed only slightly less vacuous than the pack of slobbering hounds who had run of the once elegant family townhouse. The earl had to shake his head at that name—it wouldn't be at all surprising to find the fellow gnawing bones if one called at suppertime. Even now, he fairly barked when nervous or taken by surprise.

That left three possibilities. Sheffield ran his hand over his lean jaw as he contemplated them. It would help considerably if he knew exactly what wrongdoing they were suspected of. Firebrand had been deliberately vague, hinting only that one of the men was, in all likelihood, guilty of a most dastardly deed. He knew none of them well enough to make a judgment as to whether that was possible, but there were several odd things that had popped up in regard to the second name on the list. To his mind, that was the gentleman who appeared the most likely candidate. Removing a thin cheroot from his desk drawer, the earl lit it and

slowly blew out a series of swirling rings that floated
up toward the carved acanthus-leaf molding.

There were any number of ways to delve into the
fellow's life—and that of the other two men—that he
hadn't yet tried. However, for now he would simply
send on to Firebrand what information he had gathered and wait for more specific word on what he was
looking for.

The reply that arrived the next afternoon was not
at all what he expected. Once again, Sheffield was
moved to profane language on scanning the contents
of the letter. "So I have done quite enough and am
to back off and not get any more involved!" he muttered. The paper was balled up and tossed on the
carpet, where his polished Hessian gave it a swift boot
for good measure. "It might be dangerous, he says,"
continued the earl through gritted teeth. "Well, what
does the old fellow think *he* is going to do about it.
Dangerous, indeed! I imagine I have a great deal more
experience in this sort of thing than he has." Now that
his sense of justice had been piqued, he'd be damned
if he would abandon something that obviously meant
so much to his friend.

Still fuming, he crossed to his desk and took a seat.
But instead of giving rein to a flare of emotion and
penning a heated answer, he caught himself and let
his temper cool down to a low simmer. Perhaps it
would be best not to alert Firebrand to the fact that
he had no intention of abandoning the matter. No,
rather than give away any inkling of what he intended
to do, he would simply continue the investigations on
his own. Firebrand might have no small skill with
books and words, but Sheffield was sure that he would
have a great deal more success in ferreting out what
needed to be known than his learned friend.

A grim smile of satisfaction spread across his face.
Whether Firebrand liked it or not, the earl was going
to help him right whatever wrong had been done.

*   *   *

"Are ye sure, Missy?" Jamison ran his hand through his carrot-colored hair, leaving it standing in spiky disarray. "I cannot say that I like the idea above half."

Augusta pulled her mount to a slow walk so that his horse could draw abreast of hers. It was still rather early and the park was nearly deserted, save for a few gentlemen letting loose with a good gallop on the other side of the Serpentine. "Well, I don't like it above three-quarters, but I see no other way to proceed," she answered.

"I could go by meself," ventured big footman, who had replaced her usual groom this morning to ensure the opportunity for a most private conversation.

She eyed his broad shoulders and thick chest. "You would never fit through the opening I have in mind."

Jamison could think of no argument to that. "Sweet Jesus, if Mister Edwin were here, he would like as tan my hide fer allowing ye to think of—"

"Well he isn't and he can't," snapped Augusta. They rode on in silence for a few awkward moments. "Are you going to help me or not?"

His injured expression only deepened. "As if ye have to ask, Missy. Think I'd let ye hare off on this by yerself? Not bloody likely!"

"I knew I could count on you."

"Aye, 'cause I'm the only one as daft as ye," he grumbled. "What ye need, young lady, is a husband to—"

"Oh, don't *you* start on that, too!" Under her breath she added, "The way everyone goes on about it, one would think a female simply can't live without one. If they are so important, then why doesn't the good Lord just pop us out with one already legshackled on?"

Jamison ducked his head so she couldn't see the laughter creasing his leathered face.

She gave a sigh, then returned to the matter at hand. "It may take several days to discover what evening the gentleman is planning to be away from home. Then, we shall—"

The sound of an approaching rider caused her to fall silent. A large black stallion, his coat glistening from exertion, tossed his head in the air, clearly unhappy at being reined to a sedate pace.

"Good morning, Miss Hadley." The earl tipped his curly brimmed beaver hat in greeting.

"Good morning, Lord Sheffield," replied Augusta politely, determined for once not to be uncivil. "It is a pleasant morning for a ride, is it not?"

"Indeed."

"However, it looks as though we might get a spot of rain in the afternoon."

He slanted a sideways look at her and chuckled. "It's devilish work, isn't it, trying to be polite on an empty stomach."

Augusta fought to control the twitch of her lips.

"You have an excellent seat," he said after a moment, taking obvious care to follow her lead in mouthing the standard platitudes, though there was a gleam of amusement in his eyes. "I take it you enjoy riding?"

She nodded as she watched him control his high-strung mount with casual ease. "You appear to be quite at home in the saddle as well, my lord, though it looks as if your horse is not best pleased at having his exercise curtailed."

A dark brow arched up. "Ah, a subtle hint that I have overstayed my welcome?"

Actually, it hadn't been. Augusta looked a bit startled. "I—"

"A shame. We still haven't gotten around to discussing those books yet. But then again, perhaps we should actually get through one encounter without facing off with, say, lemonade at ten paces." He tipped his hat and gave the stallion his head.

Jamison eyed the bruising rider fast disappearing around a bend, then the young lady's face, where a stain of color was fast rising to her cheeks. His own

brow arched ever so slightly, for in all his years with
the family, he had never seen Augusta affected in the
least by any male presence. "Hmmm."

Augusta jerked her head around. "What?"

The big footman quickly schooled his features into
a bland expression. "Why, nothing." He cleared his
throat. "And who might that gentleman be?"

There was a moment of ominous silence. "That,
Jamison, is the Earl of Sheffield—a gentleman more
irritating and insufferable than most." With that, she
urged her mount into a rousing gallop, making certain
to head in the opposite direction from the black stallion.

The scowl on her face only deepened on arriving
home and finding no letter addressed in the bold, familiar script awaiting her on the silver tray by the
front door. She took up the freshly ironed newspaper
and made do with perusing the latest news from the
Peninsula while picking at her toast. The pages were
turned in a leisurely manner when suddenly there was
a choking sound.

"Gus!" cried Marianne in alarm as she entered the
breakfast room. "Good heavens, are you alright? Shall
I summon Tompkins to give you a thump on the
back?"

Augusta's face, more purple from anger than from
any danger of expiring on the spot, appeared from
behind the newsprint. "He's done it again!"

"*Who* has done *what*?"

Augusta swallowed hard. Marianne knew that she
penned anonymous essays for Pritchard, but no one,
not even her sister, had any idea that she and the
controversial Firebrand were one and the same. And
it was best left that way. "No need to call for assistance," she muttered. "The only thing stuck in my
throat is the fact that the Earl of Sheffield has made
another speech on child labor in Parliament. You
know it is an issue I have a great interest in, and I
cannot help but wonder why he has chosen that, of
all topics, to make sport of."

Marianne sat down. "May I see what you were reading?"

Augusta passed her the offending page and fell to finishing her cup of tea, unmindful of the fact that it was now barely lukewarm.

After several minutes, her sister looked up in consternation "Why, it does not appear as if he is being anything but sincere. After all, why would he subject himself to such scathing criticism if he did not believe in what he was saying?" She looked down again at the printed column. "You have to admit, the reaction of his peers has hardly been encouraging, to say the least."

"Hmmmph."

"And he voices a number of the same opinions that you yourself have stated."

Augusta's cup came down rather hard on her saucer. "I sincerely doubt the earl and I agree on . . . anything."

"Well, it also seems that he has been reading the pamphlets of Firebrand. Surely you have no complaint with that man's ideas or commitment, since he is accorded to be the most articulate and provocative reformer in all of London."

Augusta managed not to fall into a paroxysm of coughing.

"And don't tell me you haven't read them, for I'd never believe you. Anyway, I've seen them hidden under the papers on your desk. All of them. And I've read enough to know he is a very gifted thinker." She lowered her voice. "Pray, just make sure Mama never hears that either of us has read such unsuitable material for innocent females else she'll take to her bed for a week to recover from the shock."

"You can be sure *I* shall never mention that name," replied Augusta faintly.

To her great relief, the subject was put to rest by the entrance of said parent, and the rest of the breakfast time was spent in going over the latest invitations and obligations for the coming week. For once, Augusta made no show of dismay at hearing the list of routs and balls she was expected to attend with her sister. How better to discover just what evening a certain lord might be absent from his townhouse?

"Are you sure I cannot fetch you anything else? A cup of chamomile tea? A cold compress?"

Augusta pulled the coverlet even higher up over her chin. "No, nothing," she croaked. "This abominable headache will no doubt disappear if I merely lie still for a time."

Marianne bit her lip as she peered into the darkened bedchamber, the heavy silk of her elegant ball gown rustling against the half closed door. "I hate to leave you alone in such distress. After all, you are never—"

"Don't be a peagoose. Peace and quiet is just what I need. Go on and enjoy the evening. I shall be just fine."

"Well, if you are sure," said her sister hesitantly. "I will look in on you when I return home."

"*No!* That is, I should prefer you didn't chance waking me. A restful night will have me back on my feet again by morning, I promise."

"Very well. Good night then. I shall leave word downstairs that you are not to be disturbed." Marianne pulled the door shut very carefully and tiptoed down the hall.

As soon as she heard the carriage conveying her sister and her mother to the Rockhams' ball pull away from the townhouse, Augusta threw off the covers and bounded to her feet. Her movements were even quicker than usual, due to the fact that she was unfettered by layers of muslin and petticoats, but rather dressed in a simple cambric shirt and rather snug dark pantaloons purloined from an old trunk of her brother's belongings tucked away in the attic. Over this ensemble she draped a heavy black cloak, then added a nondescript cap that served to hide her mass of curls. After a moment of hesitation, she rummaged in her drawer and took out a pair of black kid gloves. They made a nice touch, she thought. She added a few hairpins to her pocket, then slipped quietly out of her bedchamber and made her way down the back stairs to the scullery door.

Jamison regarded the shrouded figure in front of him with a baleful look. "Mind you, this is a good deal more serious than filching apples from Squire Havelock's orchards," he grumbled. "If things go amiss, it will be a hell of a lot more difficult fer me to haul ye out of the suds."

"Oh come on, don't turn missish on me now. Where is your spirit of adventure?"

"It must have fallen out of me cockloft, along with what little brains I used te possess."

Augusta put her hands on her hips and fixed him with a indignant glare.

"Awright, awright," he muttered. "If ye insist on going through with this, let's get on with it."

"You've mapped the quickest way through the alleys?"

"Aye, and made sure that the gate to the garden is unlocked. The watch passes by every half hour, so you've got to be in and out quickly. You are sure you can get the window open?"

She pulled the thin folding knife from her sleeve. "Don't worry. Edwin taught me how to work a latch."

"And yer sure the gentleman will not be at home?"

"Yes. I've told you, I heard him say just last night he wouldn't miss the mill taking place somewhere out past Houndslow Heath for anything in the world. And you know gentlemen and prizefights—they will all be drinking well into the next morning. It would be a wonder if any of them can find his hand in front of his face, let alone his carriage to return back to Town before this time tomorrow."

Her mouth tugged down at the corners as the

thought of who else would undoubtedly be joining in the betting and carousing came to mind. She shook her head slightly to banish the image of those blue eyes and the chiseled lips, twitching with dry amusement, as she had seen them last. But this was hardly the time to be thinking of such things, she cajoled herself.

Jamison hitched his broad shoulders. "Well then, I suppose we had better be off." By his tone one would have thought they were setting off for a funeral.

She said as much.

"Aye, and I should be carrying a spade te bury yer reputation."

"You know, if you can't say anything positive, then perhaps you should keep your mummer closed."

The big footman clamped his jaw shut, and with a sniff, set off down the darkened path.

Despite his obvious disapproval of the plan, he had been diligent in his preparation. The two of them made their way quickly through the neighboring mews and alleys, and soon arrived halfway down a narrow passage between two of the smaller limestone townhouses on a quiet street. A leafy beech tree on the other side of the brick wall afforded some measure of protection from casual observers, and as Jamison took hold of the iron gate, it swung open slightly with nary a squeak.

"In here, Missy," he whispered. "The garden is overgrown, so stay right behind me so's ye don't catch yer foot on something." He made it sound that if she did, she might fall all the way through to China.

She was right on his heels, following around until they were close to a set of tall, mullioned windows overlooking a small fountain sculpted in the shape of a carp, now nearly entwined from head to foot with climbing morning glory vines. "Ye think a fancy toff like him could afford a gardener," muttered Jamison, then his gaze moved up to the granite sill, set nearly six feet off the ground. "Here now, I'll give ye a leg up."

Augusta shook her head. "No," she whispered. "We agreed it was best you stay outside and keep a careful watch on things. Remember the signal—two sharp whistles and I am to come out immediately."

"In my experience with you, the only thing that has ever come when I whistled is that damn mutt of yours, who seems te think I'm in dire need of having me face washed every time he sees me, the way his tongue goes on." On seeing her mouth begin to open, he started to move back toward the gate. "Awright, awright. But be careful."

Her attention had already turned to the set of windows. A growth of thick wisteria had crept up the stone facade, providing an easy foothold to reach the window ledge. She swung a booted foot into the tangle of vines and climbed swiftly to where she could step onto the narrow ledge. It took only a few moments for the knife blade to jimmy the brass catch. The window came open and Augusta slipped inside.

Sheffield heard a faint scraping sound and ducked behind the heavy damask draperies. To his utter consternation, he saw a shadowy figure swing in through the window and land lightly on the thick oriental carpet. Hell's teeth! It was just his bloody luck, he fumed. Of all the fancy houses in Mayfair, a burglar had to pick *this* one to break into tonight.

He watched as the fellow stole over to the heavy oak desk, squatted down, and began to fiddle with the locked drawer. In a trice, it slid open. The earl's mouth compressed in grim satisfaction. At least the scoundrel had saved him the effort of having to break into the damned thing himself. The figure removed a thick pile of papers, but rather than toss them aside to continue the search for real valuables, he surprised the earl even further by starting to peruse their contents in the dim glow of the moonlight filtering into the study. Several pages were pulled out of the stack and hurriedly stuffed into the thief's shirt.

Sheffield decided he had seen quite enough. Slowly, stealthily, he stepped out from his hiding place and advanced noiselessly up behind the unsuspecting figure. The pistol in his right hand came up hard against the back of the other man's neck.

"Stop right there, if you don't want your brains adding another pattern to the wallpaper," he whispered.

The thief froze.

"Now stand up very slowly and turn around."

The command was obeyed, but as the figure was halfway to his feet, he twisted sharply and his elbow flew out, catching the earl a hard blow square in the midriff. He doubled over, causing him to smack his knee flush on the corner of the desk. Letting out a low grunt of pain, he struggled to regain his balance, but slipped on one of the stray papers and fell forward. His assailant looked to have every intention of making a mad dash for the open window, but didn't move quite quickly enough. As it was, he ended up between Sheffield's not inconsiderable bulk and the carpet.

Though his ribs were aching and his knee throbbing, the earl had not been knocked so senseless that he failed to realize that the body squirming under him was definitely not that of a man. Not that of a boy either. And if he had had any lingering doubts, they would have been put to rest when the fellow's hat came off, revealing a mass of curls the color of—

A string of profanities burst forth from his lips, no less heated for being uttered in a dead whisper.

"Are you always in the habit of swearing in such a vile manner whenever you encounter the least little accident?"

"Only when provoked to it by unnatural females," he answered through gritted teeth.

Augusta mumbled something unintelligible.

"What?"

"I said, would you kindly get off me so I can breathe!"

"Oh." For a moment he lingered, feeling the firm roundness of her breasts pressed against his chest, and the soft contours of her thighs molded against his own before he rolled off to one side.

"Hmmph." She sat up and clamped the hat back on her head. "What the devil are *you* doing here?" she demanded, trying to keep her voice from rising several decibel levels.

Sheffield rubbed at his sore knee. "I, er, am investiga—" He stopped short. "Hell's teeth, what am I doing answering *your* questions! What I want to know is what—"

Two sharp whistles sounded.

"What the devil is that?"

"It is the sign that we'd best be leaving. And quickly."

She scrambled to her feet and stared at the mass of papers scattered over the floor. Already there were the faint sounds of footsteps coming down the long hallway. "Damnation," she muttered. "It's vital he doesn't know his papers have been searched, but there isn't time—"

Sheffield was up as well. "Make it look like a real robbery," he said quickly, yanking out several other drawers and dumping their contents across the floor. He knocked several Staffordshire figures from the sideboard, scattered the items on the desk, and stuffed a rather ugly but expensive looking silver inkwell into his pocket, along with the pistol that he had retrieved from the floor.

Augusta watched him with grudging admiration. "Why, that's really very clever of you, sir."

"Don't just stand there!" he hissed. "Pitch in."

She promptly pitched two costly Chinese vases to the floor.

The footsteps accelerated into a run at the sound of smashing porcelain.

The earl ran—or rather limped—to the door and turned the key in the lock. "That should hold things for a bit." Then he hurried toward the window, catching hold of Augusta's elbow on the way and thrusting her up onto the ledge ahead of him as if she weighed no more than a stray cat.

Two more frantic whistles sounded.

Augusta didn't waste time with the wisteria vines. She jumped, and was racing for the back of the walled garden as fast as her flapping cloak would allow before Sheffield's boots hit the ground behind her. He was soon right on her heels, barreling through the unclipped boxwoods and scraggly rhododendrons with a display of speed if not grace.

Jamison yanked the iron gate open. "Follow me!" he cried, and set off at a dead run to their right, back down the narrow alley. Sheffield lost count of how many twists and turns the fellow made, but every painful step made him vow anew to strangle the young lady if he ever managed to get his hands on her. Twice he nearly lost his footing, first on a pile of rotting cabbage, then on something he didn't care to identify. It was with some relief that he saw that they were finally stopping for a moment at the shadowed corner of a brick mews.

"What the devil—" began Sheffield between gasping for air and massaging at his aching knee.

"We ain't got time fer questions," snapped Jamison. He pointed to a gap between the buildings. "That will take ye to Half Moon Street. From there I imagine ye can find yer own way home." His hand clamped onto the neck of Augusta's cloak and pulled her none too gently in the opposite direction. "We're going this way."

Before the earl could voice any objection, they disappeared into the night.

Chapter Six

. . . . While your instincts are noble ones, my friend, I cannot help but feel rather disappointed that evidently you feel me incapable of rendering service to you. I assure you, I am not in the least put off by what you term as "danger to my person." Indeed, those who know me would find that a rather laughable sentiment. I am well able to look after myself, as you may soon see.

Furthermore. I regret that your obligations will make it necessary for our correspondence to suffer, for I shall miss both the opinions and ideas that we have come to exchange with such honesty. Mayhap it will not be for too long. But in the meantime, I, too, shall be busy . . .

Augusta removed her spectacles and rubbed at her eyes. Oh dear. She had not meant to hurt her friend's feelings, only to protect the old fellow from possible harm. But it seemed his pride was piqued on being told there might be some task in the universe beyond his powers. A typical male response. She sighed and nibbled on the end of her pen as she wondered whether to dash off a quick note in an attempt to salve the unintentional wound. In truth, she, too, was feeling a touch out of sorts at the idea of having to curtail the frequency of their correspondence.

However, on further consideration, she decided it would be best to remain tactfully silent, at least for a while. The papers hidden in her desk proved that she was on the right track. From here on, things would require even more discretion and guile. And it would be even more dangerous. She had really not anticipated how eager her friend would be to take an active part in her investigation, and it was best to keep a damper on such enthusiasm. His enigmatic words only fanned her concern. It was one thing to put herself at risk, but she simply wouldn't countenance the idea of anything happening to him. With a faint smile, she realized she had become . . . quite fond of the fellow. If he were to suffer even the slightest injury, she would never forgive herself.

Her smile turned into a grimace at the thought of bodily harm. She could still picture the Earl of Sheffield limping through the alleyways, and hear his choice selection of epithets on stepping in several rather foul things. And she thought she had heard most every colorful expression known to man from Edwin. Hah! Her vocabulary was now considerably expanded, though she wasn't quite sure when she would have a chance to employ her new knowledge. Maybe in her next meeting with him.

Unfortunately, she had no illusions that such a meeting could be avoided indefinitely. She had already cried off three evening engagements in a row, but excuses were wearing thin. As she was never prone to indispositions, the claim of a headache could only be used for so long. And no matter how close to the fire she stood, the flush on her brow lasted only several minutes.

"Gus, you had best start dressing if you are not to be late." Marianne stepped into the cozy study, her face wreathed in concern. "You are not still feeling poorly, are you? If so, I shall insist that Dr. Adams is summoned immediately, for you are never sick—"

"No, no. I am feeling fine. I shall come upstairs in a moment." It was not exactly true, for the prospect of encountering the earl was making her stomach feel slightly queasy. But it was best to get it over with.

After all, he had as much explaining to do as she had.

With a touch of irritation, Sheffield tucked the letter of a week ago back with all the others from Firebrand. Now that their correspondence had been interrupted for a time, he was reduced to rereading past missives. Damnation, he hadn't realized how much he had counted on his friend's companionship, even if it were only in the shape of a looping script on thick paper.

But he still was rather miffed at having been denied an active role in whatever the fellow was up to. He had certainly proved his usefulness by providing a wealth of information on the six suspects. Now it seemed quite unfair to be so summarily excluded. Well, that would likely change when he proved to his friend that he was thoroughly capable of furthering the investigation—perhaps even solving it for him. Yes, it would help if he could proffer some more concrete information, instead of mere offers of help. And that, he hoped, would be soon.

Very soon.

He stalked from his study, stopping in front of the cheval glass hanging in the entrance hall to make one final adjustment to the folds of his cravat. Then he took up his gloves and top hat and signaled for his butler to summon the carriage. Leaning back against the squabs, he found himself wondering yet again about how things the other night had gone so awry. He still had not quite figured out how one moment he had been in total command of the situation, only to find himself suddenly nursing a bruised body and haring about the room to help that impossible female cover her tracks.

To make matters worse, she had somehow come away with the papers while he had ended up with nothing!

He winced as the carriage hit a bump and jostled his tender knee. Well, not exactly nothing. His ribs would be black and blue for another few days, but at least his limp had become less pronounced. The impudent chit! Acquaintance with her was becoming downright dangerous. At this rate, he ought to consider adding a man from the medical profession to his staff, for who could predict what means of assault on his person she would think of next?

His mouth thinned to a tight line. And if she thought she could avoid explaining just what she was doing in that study, riffling through a gentleman's desk, she was sadly mistaken! He'd have those papers from her in short order, too, just as soon as he managed to lay his hands on the maddening young lady.

To his consternation, the thought of physical contact with her was eliciting the most strange reaction in his nether region. Damnation, he didn't even like the chit, but he couldn't seem to put out of his mind the feeling of that long, lithe body beneath his, how the swell of her firm, rounded breasts had made him want to run his palms over the soft flesh, tease the nipples into taut nubs, and make those fascinating hazel eyes look at him with some expression other than disdain—

The devil take it, what was he thinking! He stared balefully at his well-tailored pantaloons and found his anger rising along with a certain portion of his anatomy. How had he allowed such an odd female to get under his skin? It had never happened before, not with *any* female, and it was decidedly uncomfortable. He shifted once more to ease the aches and pains in his body, then sat glowering out the carriage window as the brightly lit townhouses of Mayfair reeled by. His own base urges to the contrary, he vowed that the only physical contact likely to occur between himself and Miss Hadley was if he had to wrap his fingers around that long, elegant neck of hers to squeeze out the information he wanted.

It was not in the best of moods, then, that the earl alighted from his conveyance and walked rather stiffly up the circular marble stairs into the capacious ballroom. The dancing was already in full swing, the ladies in their swirling silks and sparkling jewels gliding by in the arms of their partners. Sheffield's scowl deepened as his eyes swept over the clusters of mamas and chaperones seated around the periphery of the dance floor and caught no sight of his quarry. Taking up a glass of champagne from the tray of a passing footman, he set off to make a closer inspection.

Augusta pressed herself closer to the arrangement of weeping ficus trees. It was a fortuitous thing she had chosen to wear a gown of emerald green, she thought, though it would have been even better had it sleeves of any kind, to allow her to blend in even more. She let out her breath as the earl made his way into the card room. However, the respite was short-lived. He appeared again moments later, his expression looking grimmer than ever.

One of the words she had learned from the earl came to mind on seeing him turn in her direction. This was proving more difficult than she had imagined. Though she knew it was best to get it over with, she could not help but wish she had stayed home in bed just one more evening.

Suddenly she spied a figure passing close by her, a glass of ratafia punch in each hand. "Jamie!" she cried.

Ashford paused. "Why, good evening, Gus." A slightly perplexed smile came to his lips. "But whatever are you doing, skulking around in those trees?"

She batted her eyelashes just as she had seen Miss Denton do. "Dance with me, Jamie."

If his jaw had dropped any farther, it would have been in his waistcoat pocket. "B-but I'm bringing some p-p-punch to Cynthia," he stammered, his eyes locked on the décolleté of her new gown.

"She will survive without you for a moment," replied Augusta in a low voice as she took the glasses from his unresisting grip and put them aside, "while I may not."

Ashford looked even more confused, but he allowed himself to be dragged out onto the dance floor. Augusta breathed a sigh of relief. Bruised toes were a small price to pay for such sanctuary. Perhaps with a bit of luck the earl would fail to spot her among the capering couples and simply go away.

That hope was quickly dashed.

"I say," remarked Ashford, as he made an awkward attempt to execute a box step turn, "Lord Sheffield seems to be, er, remarking on your new style of gowns again—that is, he has been staring quite pointedly at you for the last several minutes."

She refused to look around.

"Er, he's right, you know. Can't imagine why you didn't do it sooner. The dress, I mean. Looks marvelous." His words were moving about in as disjointed a manner as his feet.

"Ah, I don't suppose you could take me for a stroll in the garden?" Augusta gave what she hoped was a brilliant smile. "I'm feeling rather warm."

His face looked to be on fire. "But I . . . I'm to dance with Cynthia next set."

"Oh, dash it," she muttered. "You were never one to abandon a friend in the heat of battle."

Ashford eyed her with concern. "You, er, haven't perchance repeated that little experiment of sneaking into your father's supply of French brandy? I thought you had decided it was an experience you did not wish to repeat—"

"Of course I'm not foxed," she snapped. "It's just that—oh, never mind."

The music was coming to an end, and out of the corner of her eye she could see a tall, dark shape moving toward them, like a storm cloud sweeping in from the North Sea.

"No need to see Miss Hadley back to her chair, Ashford," came a deep voice. Its ominous rumble reminded her of approaching thunder. "I shall make sure she is looked after."

Her friend nearly tripped in his haste to get away.

Sheffield's gloved hand came firmly around her elbow as the first lilting notes of a waltz sounded from the violins.

Augusta smiled sweetly. "Are you sure you wish to dance, my lord? I would have thought in your present condition, it might prove a bit too strenuous."

His eyes narrowed. "Oh, don't worry about me, Miss Hadley. But now that you mention it, are you sure *you* did not suffer any lasting injury when I fell so heavily on top of you?"

The color rose to her cheeks as she recalled how the earl's muscular form had molded to her every curve. "No," she said quickly, "it had no effect at all."

"Perhaps you are right, though," he continued. "Let us forgo the pleasure of a dance and, say, take a stroll in the garden."

"Ah, I would prefer to stay right here, sir. I fear I might . . . take a chill outside."

The earl eyed her gown for a moment. It was one of the ones Marianne had chosen for her, with bare shoulders and a low neckline that her sister had said suited her figure very well indeed. Judging by the look on Sheffield's face, she was by no means assured that was true. All he finally said was, "I can see why."

Augusta felt herself getting redder.

"However, we will have to chance it, for you are going to accompany me outside, Miss Hadley, if I have to throw you over my shoulder and carry you out there."

This time she actually muttered one of the rude words under her breath, but she reluctantly placed a hand on his arm and allowed him to lead her through the french doors. At least, she thought with some small measure of satisfaction, he was still walking with a slight limp. It served him right for being such an arrogant, odious, overbearing, high-handed . . . She had not come close to running out of adjectives when the earl came to a halt by a small, circular pool screened by a low trellis of climbing roses and began to speak.

"Perhaps you would care to explain your actions of the other night." He had turned to face her. Dressed entirely in black, save for the white silk cravat knotted in a perfect Trone d'Amour, with his dark brows drawn together and his arms crossed across his broad chest, he could not have looked more intimidating. She imagined that that was the general idea.

"Actually, I would not."

It was obviously not the answer he had expected to hear. For a moment he looked nonplussed, then he quickly recovered and took a step closer to her. "I'm afraid I really must insist, Miss Hadley."

She crossed her arms herself. "Oh? And just how do you plan to do that? Whips and chains? The rack and thumbscrews?"

"Don't tempt me." There was a brief pause, then he tried another tack. "I don't know what you are up to, but whatever it is, it's a dangerous game, one you have no business playing."

"Why? Because I am a female? It seems to me, my lord, that it was *I* who had the forethought to set a watchman, it was *I* who jimmied the drawer, and it was *I* who had a planned route of escape."

"*You* should not have been there in the first place." He shifted uncomfortably from one foot to another. "I had my own plans for making a quick exit," he muttered. "And I could have opened the damn drawer just as quickly as you did."

"Well, I do have to admit that idea of making things look like a simple burglary was fast thinking on your part . . ." Her words trailed off as a wide smile spread over her face. "Good heavens, sir, it *was* a burglary. Do you think our hosts realize they have invited a hunted criminal to their gala? Why, even now the

Runners are probably combing the stews, looking for you and the missing silver."

His lips twitched. "It was extraordinarily ugly. It deserved to disappear."

"Hideous," she agreed, trying her best not to laugh aloud.

"By the way, shouldn't you be making that plural?" Try as he might to remain stern, a chuckle escaped his lips at the notion of how absurd they must have appeared, in their haste to throw the study into disarray. "The porcelain was no doubt priceless."

"It was hideous as well." Her eyes were alight with humor. "But I didn't abscond with it."

For a moment their muted laughter mingled with the distant notes of the musicians. Then Sheffield became serious again. "You may not have purloined any family heirlooms, but I did see several of the papers disappear into your, er, shirt. I should like to ask you again what exactly you were doing there."

Augusta's face became a stony mask. "I should like to ask you the same question. I assume you aren't in the habit of climbing into strange houses and making off with assorted geegaws, no matter how ugly." In truth, she was just as puzzled by his presence in the study as he was by hers.

They eyed each other warily, each seeming to wait for the other to speak. Finally the earl gave a harried sigh. He had known she was obstinate, but he hadn't realized just how obstinate. Short of resorting to the methods she had mentioned earlier, it looked as if he had precious little hope of forcing any information out of her. So this time, he tried a compromise.

"If I give you—in broadest terms, mind you—an explanation, will you agree to do the same?"

Augusta pursed her lips. "I shall consider it."

He resisted the urge to stamp his foot. He hadn't done that since he was six and hadn't yet learned to charm women in general and his nanny in particular.

"Confound it, Miss Hadley. That's hardly a fair answer."

"Perhaps not, but it is the best I can do until I hear what you have to say."

He rubbed absently at his jaw. "Hell's teeth. I suppose—"

The earl's words were cut off by a violent shove from Augusta. He staggered backward. So that the heavy coping stone merely grazed his head before crashing to the ground between them. Even so, the force of the blow was enough to knock him, half dazed, to the graveled path.

Augusta quickly knelt down beside him and took his head onto her lap. "Lord Sheffield!" Her hands smoothed away the thick raven locks from his brow, revealing a nasty cut at the hairline just above his temple. "You're hurt."

His eyes fluttered open. "Yes," he muttered faintly. "I seem to be risking life and limb every time I get near you." His hand struggled to disengage one of the thorny branches of the rosebush from the lapel of his coat, which only widened the tear it had caused in the fine fabric. "Not to speak of my wardrobe. You aren't perchance in the employ of Weston, hired for the sake of increasing his trade? The fellow makes enough off of me as it is."

She had already fished a handkerchief out of his coat pocket and had it pressed up against his wound. Her other arm moved around to cradle his shoulders. Although he had recovered his wits, Sheffield found himself strangely loath to remove his head from her lap.

"Really, sir, that is most ungenerous of you! *I* did not push that stone."

He sat up abruptly, the sudden movement causing him to wince in pain. "Son of a—" He caught himself on seeing Augusta's face quite close to his. "—of a dog," he finished lamely.

Her lips quirked. "No, what you really mean to say
is goddamn son of a poxed whore."

"*What?*"

"I said—"

"Yes, yes, I heard what you said. What I meant
was, where on earth did a gently bred female ever
hear such language?"

"Why, from you, sir, when you stepped in that pile
of decayed cabbage."

There was a distinct pause. "Cabbage, eh? I thought
it was rhubarb." He slowly got to his feet and limped
over to take a look at the fallen stone. On close inspection, it was clear the mortar had been freshly chiseled away. "Hmmm."

Augusta leaned over his shoulder and saw the evidence of tampering as well. "Hmmm, nothing, my
lord. That stone did not fall by itself." Her hand
brought the handkerchief back to his forehead, which
had started to bleed again. "Have you made any recent enemies that would wish you harm?"

"Well, if you were not present and accounted
for . . ." he murmured.

She flashed him an indignant look. "I was thinking
more along the lines of cuckolded husbands or jeal-
ous mistresses."

"I'm flattered by your notion of my prowess with
the opposite sex, but as I have tried to tell you, perhaps you should not put quite so much faith in
gossip."

She had the grace to color.

A commotion at the french doors saved her from
having to make a verbal reply. Voices were raised and
a number of gentlemen, as well as several ladies,
stepped onto the stone terrace.

"I tell you, I heard a crash, Haverlock."

Augusta straightened and waved the crumpled
handkerchief. "Over here, everyone. I'm afraid there
has been a slight accident."

The group rushed en masse over to where the two

of them were standing. One of the ladies shrieked while the evening's host blanched at the sight of the earl's blood-streaked face. "Good heavens, Sheffield, what the deuce happened?"

Sheffield shot Augusta a brief warning look, then pulled a wry face and pointed to the chunk of limestone lying on the ground. "It would seem one of the stones on your roof was loose. A gust of wind must have dislodged it."

Her face betrayed no reaction to his explanation.

Lord Haverlock sucked in his breath. "Why, you could have been seriously injured!"

The earl shrugged. "Yes, well, I suppose I was lucky. No real harm done." He brushed aside the suggestion of having a doctor summoned and refused the offer of assistance back into the ballroom. "If you would kindly send around for my carriage, I think, given the current state of my appearance, I should prefer to simply leave by the garden entrance and take myself home. I've had quite enough entertainment for one night." He brushed at one of the thick smudges of dirt on his sleeve. "Good evening, gentlemen. Ah, and good evening, Miss Hadley. I thank you for your assistance."

His voice did indeed convey a note of gratitude, but the look in his eyes as they held hers for the briefest instant told her things were far from settled between them.

The valet gave a violent start at the shout of laughter that came from the tub behind the screen. His employer had taken a nasty crack on the head and perhaps his wits were seriously addled. He peeked around the corner.

"Is . . . is everything alright, my lord?" he ventured. "Perhaps I should send one of the footmen for a doctor or . . ."

Sheffield let his aching body sink even deeper in to the hot, sudsy water, then waved the man away.

"Don't bother, Tebbins. I haven't taken leave of my senses. Just set the decanter of brandy by my bedside and then you may retire."

The man looked unconvinced, but did as he was told.

As soon as his head disappeared, Sheffield let out another chuckle. "Goddamn son of a poxed whore," he repeated aloud. The chit was utterly, maddeningly impossible! But try as he might to remain extremely angry with her, he felt a grudging admiration nudging in as well. Along with her willful obstinacy, she had displayed quick thinking and a keen power of observation. At the sight of blood, she hadn't screamed or fainted, but had handled the situation with cool aplomb. And there was no question that she possessed a sharp intelligence. She hadn't failed to put two and two together just as quickly as he did, nor had she missed his signal not to say anything about the suspicious nature of the accident. On top of all that, she seemed to appreciate the dry sort of humor he liked best.

He paused for a moment in his assessment. How had he ever thought her bird-witted or boring?

Or unattractive. Somehow, those interesting hazel eyes and graceful curves were having more and more of an unsettling effect on him every time he came in proximity of them. . . . Damnation! He reached for the pitcher of cold water and doused it over his head, though perhaps it would have been best dumped somewhere lower. He'd not let such thoughts distract him from the fact that she still had given him no explanation for her unusual nocturnal activities. It was unfortunate that his interrogation had been cut short this evening, but she wouldn't wriggle out of it quite so easily another time.

But that would have to wait for their next meeting. A more immediate concern was who had pushed the stone, and why. Another chuckle escaped the earl's lips at the thought of her suggestions. It was remotely possible, he imagined, but not very likely. He had not been as, er, active as she seemed to think. In truth, he had not even looked at a woman since—why, since he had met her.

His lips pursed in thought. The only recent activity of his that had raised any heated reactions had been his two speeches in Parliament. People may have disagreed with his point of view, but that should hardly have been the sort of thing to get a fellow killed. The more he considered it, the more it made no sense— none of the pieces seemed to fit together. Giving up, he stood up to towel off, then pulled on his heavy silk dressing gown.

But somehow he couldn't shake the feeling that Miss Hadley and the papers she had stuffed down her shirt were key parts of the puzzle.

Chapter Seven

Hell and Damnation, my friend. Forgive my strong language but it is deucedly difficult trying to help you if you will not tell me all the facts! I implore you to take me into your confidence— surely I have shown that I may trusted. I feel I am close to making an important discovery that will greatly aid your endeavor, but I must know more in order to proceed.

Hah! thought Augusta with a twitch of her lips. If Tinder considered those rather tame words worthy of apology, he had obviously never come in contact with the Earl of Sheffield! Then the expression of wry humor faded as she considered his request. It was a ticklish dilemma. On one hand, he had certainly proven both his loyalty and his practical skills by tracking down the vital information she had needed. On the other, she still feared exposing him to danger. It was all very well for a tall, lean, powerfully built gentleman like Sheffield to suffer a few cuts and bruises, but in all likelihood her friend was not cut from the same cloth as the earl.

Few men were.

Another faint smile, this one more wistful than amused, flitted across her features on remembering the feel of those broad, muscled shoulders against her bare arms. The heat from those chiseled planes had seared her, even through the layers of linen and wool. She could even recall the exact shade of his eyes—a blue the color of the sky at twilight—and every intriguing curve of those sculpted lips, fascinating to look at even when they were busy mouthing some unflattering comment at her.

She squirmed in her chair. Really, the nerve of the man, to imply that she was any more at fault than he was for the injuries he had suffered in their earlier encounters. At least he had admitted she could not possibly be blamed for this latest assault on his person.

That gave her pause for thought. But who could? Despite her comment to the contrary, she, too, doubted any affair of the heart—or other anatomical part—had prompted an attempt on the earl's life. And there was no doubt that the stone had been launched with lethal intent. The question was why.

A sharp rap at the door of her study interrupted her train of thought. She pulled a face, then quickly tucked the letter into her desk, realizing with a start that she was still undecided as to how to answer it.

"Augusta!" Her mother came in without waiting for a reply to her knock. "You have a caller. A *gentleman* caller."

Augusta's face took on a guarded expression

"Lord Sheffield wonders if he might be allowed to take you for a drive in the park."

"I'm busy. Tell him to come back some other time."

Her mother's mouth began to work, but it was several moments before any words came out. "Perhaps you did not hear me correctly. I said, the *Earl* of Sheffield wants to take *you* up with him in his high perch phaeton and join the rest of the *ton* in promenading in the park. Surely you would not be so willful as to refuse such an honor and blight your dear sister's chance of making a splendid match this Season?"

Augusta was not quite sure she followed her parent's logic, but decided arguing was useless. No doubt neither her mother nor the earl would shrink at the prospect of using physical force, if need be. With a weary sigh, she straightened the papers on her desk and rose. "Oh, very well."

Lady Farnham looked down her nose at the simple slate-gray muslin day dress that her daughter chose to work in, its unadorned long sleeves bearing several smudges of ink at the cuffs, and gave a slight shudder. "Pray, go upstairs and change. And make it quick. You would not want to keep His Lordship waiting."

A short time later Augusta appeared in the drawing room, attired more properly, if not fashionably, for the outing.

Sheffield rose. "How gracious of you to accept my invitation, Miss Hadley," he said smoothly, though it was clear he saw the jut of her jaw.

Augusta bit back a retort on seeing the look on her mother's face. "How kind of you to offer, my lord," she replied through gritted teeth.

There was a flash of amusement in his eyes as he offered her his arm. She had no choice but to take it. They proceeded in silence out of the townhouse to where the earl's small tiger was struggling manfully to keep the spirited team of matched grays in check. Once settled in the driver's seat, Sheffield gave them their head and the phaeton sprang forward at a good clip.

Augusta made a point of not meeting his gaze, though from out of the corner of her eye, she couldn't help but notice the discreet patch of sticking plaster on his brow peeking out from under the thick raven locks. It prompted her to finally speak up. "I should have thought you would have stayed home in bed today, sir, after what happened last night."

"Ah, well, since it was empty save for myself, there seemed little reason."

There was an audible intake of breath. "Are we going to have another pointless conversation where we end up hurling insults at one another?" she demanded.

Sheffield guided the high-strung team through the

entrance to the park with consummate skill. "I should hope not, Miss Hadley, for we have far more important things to discuss."

She didn't answer.

The earl drove on through the normal crush to a less crowded path before slowing the horses to a sedate walk. "As I was saying before we were so rudely interrupted last night," he continued, "I think it might make sense for us to be forthright with each other."

"I am willing to listen to your explanation, my lord."

He muttered something under his breath.

"What was that? I am always interested in expanding my vocabulary."

"I think it is stretched quite far enough as it is," he growled. His hands tightened on the reins. "Dash it all, you are truly the most stubborn, willful, provoking chit I have ever encountered—"

"I thought we were not going to indulge in such childish fits of pique, sir."

His jaw clamped shut.

"Now let's get down to business. Are you going to tell me what you were up to in that study? If not, then let us not waste each other's time and drive me home at once."

For a moment she thought he was going to urge his team into a dead gallop. Instead, a reluctant smile toyed on his lips. "I have to admit it is rather refreshing to be around a female who is not coy about what she wants."

"Lord Sheffield, I am not the least interested in your preferences regarding a lady's deportment!"

"That's quite obvious." His hand came up before she could snap out another retort. "Very well, very well. I don't suppose I have any other choice. Er, do I?"

Her scowl answered that question.

"I thought not." He cleared his throat. "Recently, I have come to suspect that a certain gentleman is

involved in some very unsavory doings. I was attempting to, er, verify my suspicions when you appeared and caused things to go awry."

"*Me!* You were the one clumsy enough to fall and
cause such a racket as to raise the dead—" She
stopped in mid-sentence. "How did you come to be
suspicious of the gentleman in the first place?"

"That's not important. What matters right now is
what *you* were doing there. I've been forthcoming,
Miss Hadley. Will you be the same?"

Augusta stared down at her lap where her hands
were balled together into a tight fist. After a considerable silence, she let out a sigh. "I am looking into
a . . . crime committed against one of our tenants at
home." That was close enough to the truth, she decided, without revealing the whole.

"A crime? Why haven't you simply gone to the
authorities?"

"Because the authorities don't give a fig for a lowly
tenant, in case you haven't noticed! But then again,
you've probably been too busy with other pursuits to
have a care for how those less fortunate live."

He flushed slightly, but didn't respond to her harsh
words. Instead, he asked quietly, "Can't you voice
your concerns to . . . some male member of your
family?"

"My father is away indefinitely in Vienna and my
brother is dead!" She sought to control the tremor in
her voice. "I'm the only one who can help."

Sheffield was silent for a moment. "Did you learn
anything definite from the papers you took?"

"I'm not sure," she admitted. "There are certain
accountings which look rather incriminating to me, but
the way they are written, it would be hard to say they
are conclusive evidence."

"Would you let me have a look at them?"

She hesitated.

His jaw tightened and he felt a sudden flare of anger
at having his offer of help spurned by yet another

person whose opinion he cared about. "I see," he said with some asperity as he made ready to turn the phaeton around. "It seems that in addition to being stubborn, willful and provoking, you are also opinionated, unbending, and unwilling to accept that you may be wrong about anything. Come, I will take you home."

Augusta's hand reached out to stay the reins. "Lord Sheffield, why is it you are taking an interest in all of this? Why are you offering to help me?"

"Why ask? You do not wish to hear aught but what may reinforce your own smug assumptions."

She was startled to hear the raw edge in his voice, as if she had scraped some vulnerable spot. "I . . . that is, if I have truly been so blind and stupid, then I deserve your scorn, sir."

His head jerked around in some surprise.

"Please accept my apology," she went on in a near whisper. "I suppose you are right and I have been just as guilty as those I rail at. I shall try not to be so quick to judge in the future." She drew in a breath. "But you must understand that my reluctance to discuss this matter stems not from any disrespect for you, sir, but from a desire not to expose anyone but myself to whatever danger there might be. Since I believe the person responsible for these crimes is a gentleman of some rank, I am well aware that I must be very, very careful who knows of my suspicions—any misstep or slip of the tongue could ruin all efforts to bring about justice, and perhaps even put those who have helped me at risk."

"I am glad to see you show that much sense at least. However, you may rest assured I can take care of myself." The earl's tone was still a bit strained, but the rigid set of his features had softened somewhat. "Who else knows about what you are up to?"

"I've spoken only to my sister and Jamison about it." That, she told herself, was not actually a lie. Though she had decided to reveal certain things to

the earl, her correspondence with Tinder she meant
to keep secret from anyone.

"I suggest you keep it that way. You are quite right
in believing that this is no mere game." He regarded
her intently. "You know, it seems to me there is a
possibility that, for whatever the reasons, we are in
pursuit of the same criminal. It might be to both our
advantages not to be at daggers drawn and to share
our information."

Augusta's lips compressed in a tight line, then she
made what she hoped was not a foolish decision. "If
you are coming to the Turnbridges' ball tonight, I shall
bring the papers."

"Thank you, Miss Hadley," he said quietly.

Some other words sounded under her breath.

"What was that?"

"I said, I hope I shall not live to regret this," she
said in a louder voice.

The corners of Sheffield's mouth twitched upward.
"May the Good Lord turn me into a goddamn son of
a poxed whore if I give you any such cause."

Augusta scanned the crowded room yet again, wondering whether the earl had succumbed to second
thoughts about the whole matter, when a low voice
sounded close by her ear. She started, nearly spilling
the contents of her glass.

"I took the precaution of approaching from the
rear," said the earl with a chuckle.

"Coward," she replied, though there was little sting
to the word.

He nodded toward the open set of double doors.
"Shall we take a stroll?"

"As long as this time we stay well out of range of
falling projectiles."

"I'll not argue with you over that. I would prefer
the precious few parts of my anatomy still unscarred
to remain that way."

Though resolved to say nothing that might be considered provoking, Augusta couldn't help but murmur, "I'm sure to you they are precious indeed."

He only chuckled again, low and so close to her ear that she could feel the warmth of his breath on the nape of her neck. "Why shame on you, Miss Hadley. Are you thinking improper thoughts?"

It was she who was put to a violent blush.

He guided her out the doors and down a graveled path toward the center of the garden. "By the way," he continued, appearing to take no notice of her flaming face, "I seem to recall having failed to thank you for last night. My headache might have been a great deal more severe had you not acted so quickly."

"If you had been left with any head at all."

"Yes, well, that is one of my parts that I would like to see stay attached, even if you do not seem to think it contains anything of value within it."

"I . . . I thought we were going to try to avoid provoking each other."

"Ah, but I cannot help finding you . . . most provocative, Miss Hadley."

"*Lord Sheffield—*" she began.

He held up a gloved hand. "Pray, don't fly up into the boughs. I am just teasing you." As they came to a wrought-iron bench framed on three sides by a tall boxwood hedge, he paused. "It appears we might have a bit of privacy here."

Augusta was intensely aware of the heat from his muscled thigh as he took a seat beside her. Good Lord, she chided herself, what was wrong with her that she was blushing and stuttering and making a fool of herself like some flighty schoolroom miss? She opened her reticule with a decided snap and began to rummage through its contents.

"Getting right down to business again, I see." His arm had come up to rest on the back of the bench and she could feel the brush of the soft wool against the silk of her gown.

"Why else would we be out here?" she snapped.

Her fingers finally found the folded sheets of paper and she handed them over. He slipped them into his coat pocket but made no move to rise.

Augusta brushed at a stray curl that had fallen near her cheek. "I have been thinking a good deal about who might wish you harm, sir. Do you still believe we may eliminate disgruntled husbands or lovers?"

The earl nodded.

"Well, that should narrow the field of suspects considerably," she said dryly.

He choked down a bark of laughter.

"I assume you don't cheat at cards or welch on your vowels, so we can ignore that line of inquiry as well. So, the most obvious thing is to assume that your recent speeches may have done more than ruffle a few feathers."

There was a gleam of grudging approval in his eyes. "That's very astute of you, Miss Hadley. I'm impressed by the power of your logic."

"I should hope I am not quite as witless as you have been wont to think," she mumbled, once again chiding herself for letting a casual compliment throw her insides in a tizzy, as if she were no more that the greenest of girls rather than an over-the-hill bluestocking.

"It's been some time since I thought that," he replied softly. His expression turned rather inscrutable before he went on. "I must admit that I have come to the same conclusion—unless, of course, the stone was meant for you."

She started. "For *me*?"

"I am not trying to frighten you, merely point out that if you continue to break into houses, purloin papers, and the like, someone may take it amiss. As you said this afternoon, this investigation of yours could turn out to be very dangerous."

"I am aware of the risks involved, my lord. But I don't frighten easily."

"No, I don't imagine you do." There was a brief

pause. "Now, let me exercise my own intuitive powers, if I may. Since the odds of our chance encounter being simple coincidence seems slim, I must assume that certain evidence has led both of us to suspect the same man."

Augusta gave a slight nod. "Go on."

"Well, as that is the case, perhaps it would be more efficient if one of us takes over from here, keeping the other person informed, of course, as to what information is discovered—"

"That 'someone' being yourself?"

"Well, er, yes." He shifted slightly. "However, you would have to tell me exactly what crime you suspect the gentleman we seek is guilty of, and why, so that I may know just what it is I am trying to help you prove."

She thought for a moment. "What sort of crime do you think him guilty of?"

The earl sidestepped the question. "I am looking into his affairs at the behest of a . . . friend."

"Why?" she persisted.

He drew in a breath. "I am not at liberty to say right now." He forbore to add that it was because he did not know the full details himself. "You are not the only one who wishes to be careful in this matter."

"So you are offering to take all the risks and share with me what you learn?"

"Yes, I suppose I am."

"Once again, I must ask why." The corners of her mouth crooked upward. "It is not as if we are even . . . friends, sir."

"No, but as I have told you, Edwin and I were."

At the mention of her brother's name, Augusta's throat suddenly became very tight. "I—" The crunch of gravel and the faint trill of laughter warned of the approach of another couple. "I must think on it."

"Do."

She got quickly to her feet. "We had best be getting back, lest people begin to get the wrong idea."

He rose as well, a slight smile on his face. "Afraid your reputation shall end up shredded by the gossips?"

"Oh, it is not *my* reputation I am worried about, my lord, it's yours," she said over her shoulder as she started up the path. "Imagine how much your consequence would suffer at your clubs and other . . . establishments if word were to get out that you'd been keeping company with an aging antidote."

Marianne scrunched up her face in a scowl.

"Don't do that," murmured Augusta. "You'll end up with wrinkles around your eyes, just like Mrs. Winslow."

"Mrs. Winslow has been making that face for nearly sixty years, so I imagine I have a good way to go before I need fear such a dire consequence." She kept her gaze riveted on Augusta and closed the book in her lap. "You are keeping something from me, Gus. And don't say you aren't, for you know I can always tell."

Augusta squirmed slightly under her sister's scrutiny. "It's not anything you need concern yourself with. Really." She cleared her throat and tried to steer the conversation away from her recent behavior. "Did you enjoy last night? Viscount Andover seemed particularly attentive and—"

Her sister let out a single word.

"I, er, wasn't aware you were familiar with that expression."

"You weren't the only one to overhear Edwin when he was angry." Marianne's scowl deepened. "And don't try to change the subject. I want you to tell me whatever it is that has you muttering under your breath more than usual. Maybe I can be of some help."

Augusta gave a reluctant laugh that turned into a wry grimace. "The Earl of Sheffield, for one thing."

"I thought the two of you had agreed to stay at arm's length."

"I'm afraid we have lately been a good deal closer than that," she murmured, a warmth stealing over her on recalling the feel of his muscled limbs and the faint, woodsy scent of his lean cheek.

Marianne stared at her with dawning horror. "Good heavens! You aren't going to tell me that the other night was no accident and it was *you* who beaned him with the paving stone?"

"Of course not! I would never stoop to such a cowardly act."

"Actually, that's right. You would face him square on and hurl it dead at his forehead."

"I wouldn't miss, either. But in this case, it really was an . . . accident." She began to fiddle with the pen on her desk. "Besides, he is—" Her words cut off abruptly. "Lamb, I really think it is best if you pay no attention to what is on my mind and go about enjoying your Season." A fond smile flitted over her lips. "It's clear you shall have your choice of—"

The spine of the leatherbound volume nearly split in two as it bounced off the floor. "Why, that's quite the most odious thing you've ever said to me in your life!" cried Marianne with some vehemence, springing to her feet and almost toppling the delicate gilt chair into the fire in the process. The shade of crimson mottling her cheeks was a perfect match of the embroidered cherries on the sash of her stylish day gown. In truth, the gown would have looked even more elegant had a good deal of it not been scrunched within two fists. "That you would tell me to run along and play while you are faced with a difficult problem is outside of enough. I'm eighteen, not eight, and while I'm not as learned as you, I am not entirely lacking in wits. Let me help."

Augusta's face turned ashen. "You know I didn't mean it that way," she said in a shaky voice. "What I meant was, I don't want to involve you in something that could prove . . . dangerous in any way. If my reputation suffers, it hardly matters, but I should never forgive myself if I caused any hurt to you." Her mouth quirked slightly upward. "And neither would Mama."

Her sister appeared a bit mollified by the explanation, but she continued to pace up and down in front of the hearth. "You needn't be like everyone else and treat me as if I were a piece of delicate china. I'll not chip or crack at the slightest knock." Her eyes narrowed in sudden suspicion. "And just what did you mean by 'dangerous'? Now that I think on it, Jamison has been going about with an air of martyrdom that usually means you have done something particularly outrageous. Just what have the two of you been up to?"

Augusta hesitated.

"Out with it. And don't forget the part about Lord Sheffield."

"Sheffield! How did you know about—" She bit her lip at the triumphant gleam in her sister's eye. "Lord, since when did you learn to extract information in such a devious, underhanded fashion?"

Marianne repressed a smug smile. "Why, since watching you in action. Anyway, it was hardly difficult to guess that something has been going on. First you are going at it with him like cats and dogs, then suddenly he is calling on you for afternoon drives, and escorting you for lengthy walks in moonlit gardens. You have to admit, it looks extremely havey-cavey."

"Maybe he is smitten with my person."

"Well, I admit that could be a distinct possibility. But what made me suspicious was not his actions, but yours. You actually agreed to go with him."

A burble of laughter escaped Augusta's lips. "I shall never underestimate your deductive reasoning again." A sigh followed. "Very well. I suppose I had better tell you the whole of it."

The lengthy story was interrupted by more than a few exclamations, accompanied by a battery of dark looks. "I can't believe you fobbed me off with that story about a headache," exclaimed Marianne when it was finished. "I should have known!" She gave her skirts another yank as she turned to face the desk. "Were you truly not going to tell me about those papers you took?"

"Well . . ."

"How could you think of concealing their existence from me! You know I was of some help in putting together the list in the first place. Let me see what I can make of them."

"I can't." As her sister's mouth fell open to protest, she explained, "I gave them to Sheffield."

"Oh." A speculative look came to Marianne's cornflower-blue eyes. "I see."

Augusta gave a slight cough. "Well, he was actually rather helpful in the library. And since the information I need to learn now can be obtained much more easily by a gentleman, I suppose I may as well try to make some use of the earl."

"I see."

"I mean, he has shown he isn't put off by a few little knocks and scratches, and it also seems that he is not entirely lacking in sense."

"I see."

"Stop saying that," she muttered while making a show of rearranging the papers on her desk.

Her sister turned to hide the slight smile that crept across her delicate features. "I must say, I am glad that you have finally discovered that a handsome, titled gentleman may be of some use. He waltzes quite nicely, too."

Augusta's face turned not quite as red as the cherries, but close. The muttering under her breath was barely audible, but the sound of the pen snapping in her fingers made a distinct crack. "Does he? I hadn't noticed."

It was Marianne's turn to laugh. "Now don't fly up in the boughs. I am just teasing you."

"Yes, well, everyone seems to have taken a notion to do that lately. I wonder why that is?"

"Perhaps it is because you tend to be so serious all the time. There's nothing wrong with enjoying yourself once in a while, Gus. Like when you are dancing with an attractive gentleman."

Augusta tried to banish all thoughts of the earl's long fingers pressed at the small of her back, the breadth of his shoulders, and the flash of his intriguing eyes. "I have a lot to be serious about," she said in a low voice. "There are still three missing children, and more are likely to suffer unless we can learn for sure who is to blame."

Chapter Eight

. . . . So that is what I think of the Earl of Sheffield's latest speech. I should like to hear your opinion, though I fear that for some reason, you still look at his efforts in a harsh light. Perhaps you have been listening to rumors rather than his actual words . . . He paused, realizing he was in danger of revealing too much, and after a moment's reflection, quickly finished off that train of thought. *My experience, especially lately, has been that outer appearance may fool you.*

But enough on that. Though you have cried off on our correspondence for a time, I am hoping that you might choose to confide in me a bit more concerning your investigation. I have made some further discoveries on my own, but it is difficult to judge their significance until I know the whole. He paused again, pen hovering above the thick vellum. *Even if you choose not to trust me, I am hoping you might consent to dashing off a quick note just to let me know you are well. You know, with your sage advice, gentle criticism, and quiet encouragement, you have become the truest friend I have. Quite simply, my dear Firebrand, I miss our comfortable correspondence and hope it may resume soon.*

A simple signature was scrawled across the bottom of the page, then the letter was set aside on a silver tray. The writer continued to stare at it, lost in deep thought, until the gilt clock on the mantel began to chime the hour. Jarred out of his reverie, Sheffield took several other sheets of folded paper from his desk drawer and tucked them into the pocket of his bottle-green evening coat. After sending word for his coach, he rose and left the room.

The Flaversham ball was, as might be expected, a great crush, given the family's wealth and position in Society. That Lady Flaversham was also known for her imaginative decorations and sumptuous suppers only made it more difficult than usual to negotiate the crowd seeking to make its way up the circular marble staircase. The earl was tempted to turn and retreat to the quiet of his club, for this was just the sort of evening he had come to consider tedious in the extreme. But he had promised he would be there.

His eyes began to scan the perimeter of the room, knowing he would be likely to find her seated with the aging mamas and retiring chaperones. Or hidden behind some damn pot of greenery. Somehow the thought of that caused a faint twitch of his lips. Miss Hadley was certainly a most unusual young lady, with a knack of turning up in the most unexpected places.

A flash of teal caught his eye. The willowy shape moved in a quick graceful arc past his nose, but not before he recognized the shape of the cheek, the wheaten color of the hair.

Damnation! The chit said she rarely danced. So what was she doing out there?

He watched her circle the floor with her partner, his mood growing darker by the moment even as he was forced to admit that her movements were a pleasure to watch. In fact, he couldn't seem to pry his gaze away from her long neck and creamy shoulders, bared by yet another lovely gown that took every inch of advantage of her magnificent body. And neither could he ignore the firm hand cupping her slender fingers or the well-formed chest leaning in much too close to her breasts.

"Good Lord, Sheff, what was that you just said?"

"Nothing," he growled, turning to face his friend.

Hobart stifled a grin. "Best remember we're not in some gaming hell or other establishment. Here, the females would faint dead away at hearing such language."

"Hah," he remarked under his breath, his eyes for a moment stealing back to the sight of Augusta in the arms of her partner.

"What has you in such a pucker? Some encroaching mama try to corner you with her young innocent?" He shook his head. "Though I can't imagine any of them would have the nerve to try that on you."

The earl didn't answer.

"Come, what say we roll that black look off your face with an evening of dice at the tables, followed by a visit to a new place I've discovered off St. James's." He lowered his voice to a discreet whisper. "The ladies are as skilled as they are lovely—it will not be your face that is growing longer by the second once we get there."

"I have some matters to attend to here."

Hobart pursed his lips. "You know, Sheff, forgive me for saying so, but you've been acting deucedly strange of late. What has happened to your sense of adventure, your devil-may-care attitude? Why, we used to always be able to count on you to come up with some crazy scheme or other."

"Have no fear," Sheffield muttered. "I am not only still crazy, I think I may be insane." The music had come to an end. Leaving his friend looking thoroughly perplexed, the earl walked off toward a quiet nook near the card room.

"What were you doing out there?"

Augusta lifted her eyes. "Since I know you are not a complete imbecile I shall refrain from answering that I was dancing."

"You said you hardly ever dance."

"I danced with you." She paused a fraction, as if

considering the matter. "Ah, but of course that was different. . . ."

He looked as if to speak.

"You forced me. The other gentleman did not."

His brows drew together in an ominous line. "Miss Hadley—"

"I'm teasing you, Lord Sheffield. Does no one dare tease you, or are you the only one allowed to indulge in such behavior?"

"I am not in the mood tonight," he snapped. Nor, it seemed, was he in the mood to picture some gentleman's hand at the small of her back, or his artfully arranged curls bent close to hers.

"Oh? Bit of a headache? Knee throbbing? Ribs feeling a touch sore?" she inquired with feigned innocence.

"It is my patience that is frayed. Dangerously so. I should like to get down to business," he said in a scathing tone. "That is, if you are not too busy having a good time."

She folded her hands primly in her lap. "Then pray, do go on, sir."

"I think I am in need of a glass of champagne first. May I fetch you something as well?"

"Yes, thank you. I shall spend the time that you are gone thinking of something creative to do with it." She ran an appraising eye the length of his person. "Let me see, burgundy and forest green—no, a splash will never show to best advantage on your waistcoat. But the cravat has possibilities. Could not you have tied it in a Waterfall for tonight?"

The earl had to choke down a bark of laughter.

Augusta smiled on seeing his scowl disappear. "That's better, sir. It is much too intimidating trying to converse with you when you are wearing such a menacing expression."

"Why is it I have a feeling precious little intimidates you, Miss Hadley," he murmured. "Most especially not my phiz, menacing or otherwise?" He signaled to a passing footman and returned in a moment with two glasses of champagne.

"Now that you have been coaxed out of your sullens, may I ask what it was that had you looking as if you wanted to plant someone a facer?"

He took a long swallow from his glass. "I suppose I was a tad out of sorts because I was thinking of someone I have not heard from in some time." On seeing the look on her face, he made a wry grimace. "It is not *that* sort of acquaintance. It is merely a good friend, someone I trust and whose wise counsel and insight I miss."

Augusta's face became rather pensive. "I too—that is, I think I understand what you mean, sir. It is so rare that we may be honest and forthright with our feelings that to find someone with whom we can share our thoughts, with no fear of censure or ridicule, is special indeed."

The earl stared at her, suddenly wondering just what sort of thoughts were hidden behind those intriguing hazel eyes. To his surprise, he also felt a slight stab of jealousy at the lucky fellow with whom she might choose to share them.

The intensity of his gaze caused her to drop her head in some confusion. "I . . . I hope that all is well with your friend and that you hear from him soon." For a moment she studied the tiny bubbles in her glass as if wondering what odd chemistry produced such effervescence between the two elements. "I take it you have had a chance to read the papers I gave you. What do you make of them?" she asked abruptly.

He moved closer to her chair and turned his back to the line of dancers capering through a lively country dance. "I assume you are referring to the columns listing transfers, dates, and amounts."

She nodded.

"Well, he seems to be talking of wheat, corn, and rye."

"Yes, but his estate raises only sheep!" she said

with a note of barely contained triumph. "Those headings could be a code for something else. I have read of such things in . . . a book."

One dark brow arched up. "*The Dark Lord of Trieste*. Yes, I've read that one too. Really, Miss Hadley, so you *do* prowl the aisle with the horrid novels."

"I never said I didn't read them," she muttered.

He gave a slight chuckle. "Well, in this case I am afraid that wheat means wheat. You see, Wilburton has just entered into a partnership with a Cit to trade with the Americas, though he'd cut off his right hand before he would ever admit it to his friends. You saw the condition of his garden, hidden away from the public eye. His father drained the family coffers, and though he's been struggling to keep up appearances, he's in desperate need to replenish them. So, by teaming his connections with certain people in Boston with the merchant's money, the two of them have a decent chance of being successful."

"How did you find out about it?"

Sheffield paused. "Gentlemen may not reveal certain things to their friends, but they tend to talk rather freely with their ladybirds, especially at the end of the evening's activities."

Augusta's lips compressed. "Just as I thought. Men get to have all the fun—"

He nearly choked on his champagne.

"What I meant was . . . investigating interesting things."

His look of unholy amusement only increased.

She made a sound suspiciously like a snort. "Oh, do stop that, sir. This is no laughing matter." Her fingers tightened around the stem of her glass. "It seems that if you are sure we may rule out Wilburton, then I will have to figure out how to proceed with the others."

All traces of humor were quickly wiped from the earl's face. "What others?"

Her jaw clamped shut.

"I trust that does not mean you are contemplating another late-night burglary."

"Well, since some other types of inquiry seem out of the question for me, it does seem the most effective way of discovering secrets."

"It's much too dangerous. Miss Hadley, have you any idea how close you came to being caught?"

"It was only because *you* made such a racket when you tripped over the edge of the desk," she said under her breath.

"I didn't trip. If you care to remember correctly, I was pushed. Rather hard." He took a step closer, forcing her to look up at him. "In any case, a repeat of that evening's adventure is out of the question. I absolutely forbid you to consider it."

Augusta's features scrunched into an expression unbecoming to a properly bred young lady. "You do? And just how do you presume to order me about, sir? You are not—" Her words cut off sharply.

"No, I am not your brother. But I'm damn sure Edwin would have locked you in your room—or worse—had he known what sort of trouble you were courting."

Her chin came up a fraction. "Edwin would have understood that I would never abandon my friends, sir."

He gave an exasperated sigh. "I am not expecting you to do so. I told you, I am quite willing to pursue this matter, and even you have to admit that so far I have managed not to make a complete mull of it— despite being a pompous ass and indolent wastrel."

Augusta had the grace to color.

"As I have also said, I could be a good deal more effective if you would see fit to explain to me what crime has been committed."

There was an awkward hesitation before she replied. "I fear this is not the best of places to go into the whole thing, sir."

"Quite right. I shall call on you tomorrow afternoon

at three. My phaeton should afford us enough privacy for such a discussion. Does that meet with your approval?"

She nodded.

"Good." He started to move away.

"What are you doing!" Augusta suddenly found herself on her feet, the glass carefully removed from her hand and placed aside.

"I am forcing you to dance, Miss Hadley."

Before she could protest, the earl's arm was firmly around her waist, and her feet were moving of their own accord in perfect harmony with his. For a short time they danced in silence. Sheffield closed his eyes and found himself marveling at how light she felt in his grasp, how utterly unique was her scent of lavender and lemon.

"My Lord . . ."

He forced his lids open.

"I feel I must warn you once again."

"Of what, Miss Hadley?"

She drew in a breath. "Of the gossips, sir. I was not entirely in jest the other night when I mentioned that people were talking about the fact that you seem to be paying attention to me. Since no one has any notion of the real reason, it is bound to cause some discussion. In fact, I have already overheard more than one reference to it, and I should not wish to see you . . . embarrassed in any way by the connection. So you might want to avoid any further conversations in public with me, and certainly any further dances."

His lips came to within an inch of her ear. "May the gossips all be turned into goddamn poxed sons of whores, Miss Hadley."

The clock had long ago struck midnight, but Augusta still sat in her study gazing into the flickering flames, her heavy silk wrapper pulled tightly around her shoulders. Sleep had proved impossible. She couldn't help but feel her decision to take the Earl of Sheffield

into her confidence was going to prove a most dangerous one. It was not that she didn't trust him. Rather
it was her own confused reaction to him that was in
question.

Drat the man!

She didn't know quite how it had come about, but
somehow she no longer thought of him as odious and
overbearing but clever and compassionate. It was
abundantly clear he had a keen intellect as well, along
with the sort of humor and strength of character that
she could admire in a man.

Not to speak of what she felt at his physical touch.
It was as if someone was holding a match to her skin
every time his hand brushed against her. And the sight
of those chiseled lips when his face bent tantalizingly
close to hers made her mouth go dry. Why, every time
she looked at him it was becoming more and more
difficult not to imagine how it might feel if he . . .
kissed her.

At that, her own lips twisted into a mocking smile.
Well, that was not ever likely to happen. She might
harbor insane fantasies, but she was not a candidate
for Bedlam. If even half the rumors were true, the
earl had his choice of most any of the ladies—and
quite a few who were not. All of them undoubtedly
had the sort of lush feminine charms that could attract
an experienced rake. She grimaced. The only thing he
noticed about her was her sharp tongue, advanced age,
and hoydenish behavior. Now what man would want
to kiss a female who had verbally raked him over the
coals, knocked him on his rump, punched him in the
ribs, and caused him to fall into a desk? Oh, and then
of course there was the little matter of the lemonade.

Her eyes pressed closed. And that was not the half
of it. If the earl knew what other activities she was
engaged in, he would no doubt think her an even more
unnatural sort of female than he already did. Despite
his words on forming hasty judgments, it was quite
clear he thought her—or any of her sex—incapable of

reading anything more strenuous than a horrid novel, so if he ever discovered that she wrote . . .

Not a chance!

Her jaw set. He had shown he was adept at discovering certain intimate details about other people, but she would make sure he never learned *her* secret.

When the butler announced the arrival of the earl the next afternoon promptly at three, Augusta had managed to put her personal feelings well under control. She greeted him with a cool nod and allowed him to hand her up to the perch of his smartly appointed phaeton with nary an outward hint of the frisson his touch sent along her spine.

They did not speak until he had guided his team into the park and past the occasional carriage to a less traveled path. It was still some time before the fashionable hour to make an appearance, so there was no one else around them. He slowed the horses to a leisurely walk, and although Augusta had made a point of not looking at him during the trip, she couldn't help but notice the sure command with which he handled the reins. She bit her lip and forced her eyes away. There was important business to attend to. It would not do to let her thoughts start straying to what else she might like those long fingers to be touching . . .

"You are looking as though you would like to take that dainty parasol of yours and bat someone over the head with it."

Myself, she thought with an inward grimace.

Sheffield ran an appraising eye over her rigid profile, taking in the dark circles under her eyes and the tautness of her mouth. "You also look as if you have had precious little rest lately."

She flushed slightly, grateful he could not guess the cause of her sleepless night. "How gentlemanly of you to notice, my lord," she snapped. "But I have little

need of you to tell me my looks do not match up well
with those of other ladies of your acquaintance."

His brows drew together, but he refrained from any
response. Instead, he merely pursed his lips, then went
on. "I believe you were going to tell me the whole
story of the crime you are seeking to solve."

"Yes." Augusta let out a sharp sigh. "That is, forgive me if I seem on edge. I . . . I have been very
busy these days."

"No doubt," he murmured. "Doing the job of Bow
Street is deucedly hard work, as I have also discovered."

She stole a glance at him to see if he was mocking
her, but it seemed his blue eyes held only a glimmer
of sympathy, or as close to such a softer sentiment as
the earl was capable of. To mask the effect that look
was having on her insides she forced a scowl and a
sharp retort. "Harder work than being a rake?"

"Much. And the rewards are less immediate."

That drew a grudging laugh. "You are impossible,
my lord."

"Well, that is a step up from being insufferable, I
suppose." A smile twitched on his lips. "Now that I
have returned the favor of coaxing you out of your
sullens, shall we get on with the matter at hand? I
admit, I am quite anxious to know all the facts."

Augusta seemed to hesitate. "My lord, before I tell
you everything, there is still one question I should like
for you to answer. What is the real reason that you
have spoken out on the issue of child labor?"

His face hardened. "Ah, you still think it the result
of a drunken wager, or mere whim? Are my ideas so
lacking in merit that you find them a joke?" There
was no mistaking the growing edge in his voice. "It's
clear you think it unfair that people do not believe
you capable of understanding intellectual concepts or
forming opinions simply because of who and what you
are. Has it ever occurred to you that I might feel the
same?" He paused. "You want to know why I have

spoken out? Because I read things too, Miss Hadley. Does that shock you, that I am capable of turning back the covers of more than just a bed? Or is it that you think an—how did you put it—indolent wastrel could not possibly care about anything more than his next mistress or hand of cards?"

She swallowed hard, surprised as well as puzzled that he had remembered to the letter her harsh words of the past. For some reason, he seemed truly upset that she might see him as the rest of Society did, and yet she could not fathom why. "It has been quite some time since I have thought of you in those terms," she said very softly.

"Oh, and in just what terms do you think of me now?" His eyes had taken on an even more intense shade of blue.

"A . . . friend, I suppose. Because of Edwin." She twisted the pearwood handle of the parasol in her hands. "You told me before that you felt some debt to my brother, so that, I imagine, is why you are offering to help me."

"Ah yes, brotherly friendship," he muttered through gritted teeth.

"I did not mean any insult by my question, my lord. Truly I didn't. I merely want to be assured that your feelings on this matter run deep. For if I decide to take you into my confidence, I should not want to discover my trust was misplaced."

"I may appear shallow to you, Miss Hadley, but rest assured that the current of my convictions is stronger than you imagine. When I set my mind to something, I am not easily put off course."

Augusta drew in a deep breath. "Very well then, sir. The whole thing started six months ago, with the disappearance of a child from the fields near my home. That was terrible enough, but soon after, another went missing. A third was abducted just a month ago. There was sign of a struggle, and I found a scrap of expensive silk fabric nearby, the sort of material used to make up a gentleman's waistcoat."

"Do you think this certain gentleman is the sort of monster who has an appetite for murdering children? Have any bodies been found?"

She shook her head. "No. Nor do I think any will be."

His brow arched in question.

"I cannot help but think the disappearances have to do with some other reason, which is nearly as appalling. In the course of my readings, I have come across mention of how some of the mines in the north are getting child labor from unscrupulous sources— that is, children stolen from their homes." Her mouth twisted in some disgust. "It is cheap, for the owners don't have to pay even a paltry wage, and effective, for the small bodies may wriggle in where a man cannot. And it is, sir, little more than slavery."

Sheffield pursed his lips. "Have you any proof at all of this?"

She shook her head. "No, but my intuition tells me I am right." The tone of her voice indicated that she expected him to challenge the assertion.

He gave a snort, then looked as though he might.

"Before you begin what will undoubtedly be a harangue on the merits of a female's intuitive powers— or lack thereof—let me add a few other points of unassailable fact. I have done a fair amount of research into the matter and, as it happens, there are several large mines around Newcastle where the shape of the veins of coal make extraction difficult. Small bodies at work in the tiny passages are the only way to keep them profitable. And profitable they have been, but only starting about six months ago."

The earl tugged at the brim of his curly brimmed beaver hat. "The devil take it," he muttered. "It still seems to me as if you have precious little to go on."

"Hmmph." Her parasol came down on the floorboard of the phaeton with a decided thump. "And

what about falling coping stones? Someone is clearly
not happy about any stirring of public interest in the
subject of child labor. You may fail to see any connection, but the link is certainly clear enough for me."

"For you to do what?"

There was a slight pause. "I imagine if you close
your eyes and think very hard, my lord, you shall be
able to conjure up some idea of what I mean."

The oath that followed was one she decided was
well worth filing away for future reference.

"I vow, Miss Hadley, if you were my sister, I
should—"

"Well, I am not."

He continued to stare at her intently for a moment.
"Right," he said slowly. "And just how many more
suspects do you have on your list, may I ask?"

Augusta decided there was little harm in answering. "Two."

The earl's head jerked around. "Two?" he repeated,
eyeing her with some surprise. What an odd coincidence. That was exactly the same number he was
left with.

"You appear disappointed. Would you have preferred more?"

Sheffield didn't answer but continued to consider
the matter. Despite his initial skepticism, he had not
entirely dismissed her conjecture as absurd. He, too,
in the course of his readings had become aware of
such sinister doings. It was just possible she was on to
something. Yet he was determined to figure out a way
to keep her from pursuing that line of inquiry. If she
was right, she was courting more danger than even
she could imagine—not, he noted wryly, that such
knowledge would have the least effect in stopping her
head-on assault on injustice.

"Miss Hadley," he finally said, trying to keep a tone
of reason in his voice, "let us think on this a moment.
You have two more suspects. It so happens that I have

the same number in mind. Let us leave our waltzing around on the dance floor."

"Sir, I cannot believe they would be the same—"

He rattled off two names.

Augusta gave a faint gasp. "How is it that you came up with those men?"

His hands tightened on the reins and he turned his team toward an even more secluded spot. "I should have liked to keep this to myself, but I see if I am to have any hope of convincing you to let me handle this, I shall have to reveal certain things." He took a deep breath. "I have already told you that I became involved in this at the behest of . . . a friend. While you may find my intellect and commitment suspect, I doubt you would find any such fault with this learned man. Especially concerning the subject of child labor." He turned to face her. "Have you read the pamphlets of Firebrand?"

Augusta was overcome by a fit of coughing.

"Don't try to gammon me. Given your interest in the subject, I would never believe a denial."

"I . . . I am acquainted with them," she managed to whisper.

The earl lowered his voice as well. "Well, I am acquainted with the author."

"You . . . know . . . who Firebrand is?"

His lips quirked upward. "Well, I have to admit that I do not actually know his real identity. But we have corresponded through his publisher on a regular basis for some time now. He has asked for my help in pursuing a matter that I cannot help but feel is related to yours. It is from him that I have received my information, and it is on his behalf that I am acting. I should hope that would convince you to trust me. After all, it is apparent that *he* does."

Her throat became so tight she found it difficult to squeeze out a reply. "Is Firebrand aware of your identity?"

"I see no reason why he should be. We have chosen

to remain anonymous to each other for a variety of reasons." Sheffield's jaw tightened imperceptibly. "You think it would make a difference in his attitude if he knew?"

Augusta stared down at the strings of her reticule which were now twisted into little knots. "I imagine that is a question only Firebrand can answer, my lord."

"I am asking your—" He stopped speaking on noticing that her hand had come up to rub at her temple. "Are you all right, Miss Hadley? You seem to be looking a trifle pale."

"I am sorry, sir. I find I am suddenly feeling very fatigued."

Sheffield peered at her wan face and muttered an inward curse for pressing her too hard. "Come then, I had best take you home."

She made no attempt dissuade him.

The team started forward at a smart pace, the earl guiding them back through the park and the crowded streets of Mayfair with a sure hand. He slanted an occasional glance at her rigid form, but found himself only looking at the poke of her bonnet, for her averted face was shielded in its shadows from any further scrutiny.

His mouth crooked in some concern. Damnation, he thought, she was trying to shoulder entirely too much responsibility, though he could well imagine her response should he voice the opinion that she couldn't go on without help—a man's help. That caused the corners of his mouth to turn upward. His ears would be soundly boxed, if not his person, but he found he was becoming rather used to their verbal sparring. In fact, he rather liked it. Though he had never expected it, she had proven up to his weight in both giving and taking a hit. Her grit and determination were most unusual in a female—why he was almost relieved to see her admit to a bit of fatigue. It showed she was human.

He stole another quick look at the rounded curves of her willowy form, shown to perfection in a new carriage dress of impeccable design and cut.

Way too human.

The team pulled up in front of her townhouse and Sheffield quickly came around to hand her down.

"Get some rest, Miss Hadley. I trust when you have given the matter careful thought, you will use your good judgment and good sense to come to the right decision."

Chapter Nine

I am sorry, my friend, but I am involved in a certain project that requires all my thought and energy at the moment so it will be another little while before I can find my way clear to writing you anything longer than a few lines to assure you I am well.

Oh, and as to the little matter that I requested you to help with—you may rest assured that it is taken care of and there is no need for you to exert yourself in any further way. I have decided to hire two Runners to handle it, and have put the investigation entirely in their hands.

Her shaking fingers barely managed to scrawl those few lines before setting aside the pen with a sharp intake of breath that sought to control the racing of her pulse. Trying to avoid yet another glance at the latest letter that had been forwarded to her by Pritchard, she sealed the note and rang for a footman to take it away.

As the door fell shut, Augusta allowed herself to slump back in her chair. A muffled groan followed. Then another. Good Lord, she was not exactly sure how she had contrived to climb down from the phaeton and negotiate the marble steps of the townhouse without collapsing like some hysterical peagoose in a horrid novel, for her legs still felt about as substantial as blancmange.

It simply couldn't be possible!

Her eyes stole back to the bold script covering the single sheet of thick cream stationery that lay on her desk and she pressed her palms to her temples To think that the thoughtful, sensitive, and compelling author of that missive was one and the same gentleman as the sardonic, cynical, and decidedly rakish Earl of Sheffield! How apt that "Tinder" was the moniker he had chosen for his other, hidden self, for he had certainly set her world on fire.

Augusta's hands slid down to cover her burning cheeks and more than several of the newly learned oaths came to mind. It was one thing to have developed a *tendre* for someone who only existed on paper. After all, it was merely an . . . intellectual exercise. But it was quite another thing to find that the compassionate thinker whose bent of mind was so in harmony with hers was also, in the flesh, a maddeningly attractive gentleman with flashing blue eyes and a raffish smile that sent a frisson of heat spiraling deep inside her. Suddenly the passion was all too real.

She pressed her eyes closed, as if she could avoid seeing the awful truth. But brutal honesty compelled her to admit it—she was in love with him.

It wasn't as if she wished to be, but she was.

Pushing up from her chair, she rose and began to pace back and forth before the blazing fire. Each crackle and hiss of the logs seemed to echo the emotions flaming inside her. *Goddamn son of a poxed whore!* Now the question was, what was she going to do about it? It was a devilishly difficult situation, but the more she thought about it, the more one thing became very clear. The only notion more absurd than finding herself in love with the Earl of Sheffield was to imagine that he might ever feel a shred of such sentiment in regard to her.

Augusta's steps faltered as a number of his words came echoing back in her head. He had made it quite clear that the list of things that attracted him to a female did not include a brain, but rather other, more

obvious, physical attributes. In addition, he had made
reference to the fact that his vast experience with the
opposite sex had led him to form a firm opinion that
even if they had a brain, they were incapable of using
it for any meaningful endeavor. In short, he had no
use for any of them—that is, no use but one.

She swallowed hard. So he would no doubt be
shocked if it came to light that the male friend whose
opinions he held in such high esteem was . . . herself.

Actually, he would be more than shocked. He
would be furious.

If she had understood Edwin correctly, the sort of
things Sheffield had revealed to her in his letters were
intimacies that one might only discuss with a close
friend after more than a few bottles of port at their
club. She had a feeling that the same sort of silly pride
that made gentlemen aim pistols at each other from
twenty paces would make it impossible for him to ac-
knowledge that the counsel and comradery the two of
them had shared was no less real simply because she
did not wear breeches and boots—well, at least not
most of the time.

Drat Society! Drat convention! She was beginning
to feel angry in her own right, for it appeared that
something that she had come to value above all things
was going to be destroyed for no sensible reason.
Blinking back the prick of tears, she realized how
important the honesty and truth that had developed
between them had become to her, and how loath she
was to give it up. For several minutes, her half boots
beat an angry tattoo over the thick Oriental carpet,
then her steps slowed and her hand reached out to
pick up his latest letter.

As she toyed with the thick paper, taking in the
faint scent of bay rum and tobacco, it slowly occurred
to her that things didn't have to change, not if he
never learned the true identity of "Firebrand." She
might not ever be able to hope for his love, but she

had his friendship and that was equally as precious. She meant to keep it.

She began pacing with renewed vigor. Though he suspected some common thread somehow tied the two crimes together, she was sure he had not begun to guess at the real truth. The note she had just sent off in which she announced the hiring of the Runners might serve to delay any further action on Firebrand's behalf for a bit. He was too astute to be fobbed off for long, but in the meantime, she would have a chance to think of some other reason to put him off—or to solve the crimes herself.

Dealing with the earl on paper was one thing. Facing those mesmerizing blue eyes was quite another. She made another turn around the room, then paused once again before the desk. Her jaw set on edge. There was really no choice but to sever all contact with him, and the sooner the better. The waltzes, the carriage rides, the conspiratorial walks in the garden would all have to end. It was far too dangerous otherwise—for a number of reasons. She feared his deductive powers were too sharp not to eventually cut through the shroud of mystery surrounding this entire affair, leaving her exposed as the incendiary reformer. But more than that, she feared she would never be able to hide her true feelings from his penetrating gaze. Would he find it amusing that even an aging bluestocking was not immune to his charms? Or merely pitiable? That, she wasn't sure she could bear.

No, she had already revealed too much of her soul, however unwittingly, to the Earl of Sheffield. The state of her heart she preferred to keep her own little secret.

Of course there would have to be a reason to cut things off. A bitter smile played on her lips as she picked up the brass letter opener and ran her thumb along its edge. It should not be so difficult to find a reason to quarrel—after all, they had a good deal of practice in it. This time, however, she would have to make sure that, despite his feelings of duty to the memory of her brother, he was put off for good.

"Gus?" The note of concern was evident in Marianne's whisper as she took her sister by the arm and drew her aside at the entrance to the drawing room. "You look as though you haven't slept a wink all night." Her eyes narrowed. "You and Jamison haven't—"

Augusta gave a tight smile. "No," she answered. "I promise you I haven't engaged in any more nocturnal adventures. I'm afraid this time my claim to being indisposed by a headache is all too real."

Marianne's tone sharpened. "What has happened?"

"Nothing has happened save for this throbbing at my temples which you are only making worse."

"Fustian! You never have headaches. Did Lord—" Her words cut off abruptly as the ample form of Lady Thorlow sailed past them in a flutter of mauve flounced silk to join the other morning callers already clustered around the tray of cakes. Augusta made to follow in her wake, but Marianne's hand remained on her sleeve. "Don't try to put me off. Did Lord Sheffield discover anything of note in the papers you showed him?"

"Only that we may eliminate Wilburton as a suspect."

"Well, what does he suggest—"

"I have no idea, since I didn't ask." Augusta hoped her voice did not sound as brittle as it did to her own ears. "His Lordship merely filled me in on several facts that explain the contents of the papers I discovered in Wilburton's drawer. Aside from that, I have no intention of involving him any further in this matter."

Marianne did not look to be satisfied with the explanation. "But—"

A pointed cough from their mother made further private conversation impossible. With a resigned shrug, Marianne moved off to join Lady Hawley's two daughters, who were busy perusing the latest copy of

La Belle Assemblée. However, the look on her face before she turned away promised that the interruption was by no means an end to the matter.

Augusta took a seat near the tall, mullioned windows and prayed that no one would take much notice of her presence. The clink of china and the trill of voices echoed through the room, but she found herself unable to pay the slightest heed to what was being said. Instead, her gaze wandered to where the first drops of rain were running down the panes of glass and her thoughts strayed far from any discussion of the shocking color of Lady Walton's latest gown or the size of Miss Hepplewhite's dowry.

". . . I heard it was Lord Sheffield who held the poor boy's vowels. The man certainly has a reputation for uncanny luck. His winnings were over two thousand pounds in less than an hour."

There was a slight titter. "The reputation is for more than luck, my dear Honoria. But pray, what happened?"

Augusta's attention was suddenly engaged. Her head turned discreetly toward the nearby settee, where two of her mother's acquaintances were bent together in earnest gossip.

"Oh, Linton was forced home to Yorkshire in disgrace, and just when he was on the verge of making the Grenville chit an offer," replied Lady Reston.

Her friend made a disapproving cluck. "I heard the young man was obviously in his cups. Really, has the earl no scruples, making sport of mere boys?"

It was the other lady's turn to give a slight laugh. "Why, of course he has no scruples. That's what makes him so . . . interesting. Why, have you heard who his latest conquest among the *ton* is rumored to be? Lady Stansfield has not been a widow these three months and yet . . ." The voices dropped into a flurry of whispers too low to be followed, but Augusta had heard enough.

Her mouth thinned to a grim line as she let her

eyes drift back to the windows. Though the sight of the leaden skies only served to further dampen her already heavy spirits, she forced herself to consider what she had just overheard with a purely rational detachment. It would seem these latest rounds of innuendo, however specious, gave her more than enough ammunition with which to slay any lingering feelings of obligation that Sheffield might feel in regard to her.

The rest of the tedious hour she spent marshaling both the words and the resolve for an attack on his character. It should not prove so very difficult to precipitate a final quarrel. After all, through his letters she was intimately acquainted with his most vulnerable spots. While in the past she had unintentionally wounded his feelings, now she knew just where to strike with greatest effect. By the time the guests rose to take their leave, she had no doubt that after their next encounter she could make sure that the last thing in the world the Earl of Sheffield would want would be to spend a moment more in her presence.

Perhaps that was why Marianne, on taking one look at her pinched face, let her retreat to her study without further remonstrance.

The earl watched with growing impatience the shifting patterns of the country dance. Would the cursed music never end? he thought, his foot tapping the floor more in irritation than in rhythm with the melody. And would the maddening chit never sit down? Ever since she had taken to wearing those vastly improved gowns, it seemed she had no dearth of dance partners. His eyes grudgingly followed her graceful steps across the polished parquet and he couldn't help admit how utterly wrong she was about being awkward in movement, just as she was utterly wrong about a number of other assessments of her person. He drew in a deep breath, hoping that his self-control would extend down past his clenched jaw to a certain other region.

The notes did indeed finally die away and Augusta was escorted by her partner toward a quiet spot between two towering urns spilling a profusion of ivy twined with white shrub roses. The earl waited until it was clear that no other gentleman was coming to claim her for the following set before making his way to where she sat.

"It appears that you suffer from no bout of fatigue tonight, Miss Hadley." He was surprised at the note of asperity in his own voice. But even more surprising was the tightness of the delicate skin around her eyes and the drawn expression on her pale features as she slowly looked up at him. If anything, she looked even more exhausted than the day before. His irritation deepened into something more than mere peevishness. "Have you no sense at all?" he snapped. "You should be home in bed, not—"

"Yes, no doubt beds are quite on your mind these days," she retorted. "Only I should have thought it would be you who would be tucked between the sheets by this hour, my lord, not me."

His dark brows came together in an ominous line and he took a step closer to her chair. "Just what is that supposed to mean?" he demanded.

"Use your prodigious intellect to figure it out."

Sheffield's mouth compressed at the obvious sarcasm, but there was more puzzlement than pique in his voice as he studied her pale face once again. "What the devil is wrong?"

"The fact that you insist on hovering about my person, sir." Her mouth set in a prim line. "It is becoming quite tiresome."

It was his face that became a shade paler. "Tiresome?" he repeated softly.

"I should imagine you would prefer to be with Lady Stansfield or—what was the name of the opera dancer?"

"Hell's teeth, is that what is upsetting you?"

Augusta's lips curled in a mock smile. "Why in

heaven's name would that upset me, sir?" she inquired. "I couldn't care less how you choose to amuse yourself, or with whom. What I do care about is having you make sport of serious matters by pretending to care about aught but pleasure. I have no idea why you persist in trying to convince me that your concern is anything deeper than mere whim."

A flare of anger flashed in his eyes. "It is clear you have been listening to the gossips again and giving their wagging tongues far more credence than they deserve. Perhaps it is your intellect that should be ridiculed, not mine, for it appears right now that your brain is no bigger than a pea if you still insist on taking such rumors seriously."

"Well, at least I try to use my brain, however small, rather than some other parts of my anatomy. Common sense says that where there is smoke, there is fire."

The earl sought to control the sparking of his temper. "The only thing smoky is the idiotic way you are acting. I thought we had come to some understanding regarding the sorts of accusations you are hurling in my face, but evidently we have not. Come, let us take a stroll in the garden and discuss this in the rational manner I have come to expect from you."

She refused his hand. "I thought you didn't want or expect rational behavior from a female."

There were several moments of silence. "I think, Miss Hadley, that you owe me some sort of explanation for this outburst. I cannot quite believe that it has only to do with what the tabbies are bandying about."

"Believe what you wish, sir, but even you cannot be so vain as to not realize when your presence has become distasteful. Or are you truly so puffed up with conceit that you think every female is waiting for a chance to fling herself at your feet?"

His jaw worked but before he could make a reply, another gentleman approached.

"I believe we are engaged for the next dance, Miss

Hadley, but if I am interrupting . . ." His brow rose a fraction as he regarded Sheffield's rigid features.

"Not at all," replied Augusta, giving the gentleman a brilliant smile. "Lord Sheffield was just taking his leave." She extended her hand to him and there was nothing for the earl to do but step aside.

He watched them walk away to the far end of the dance floor where the next set was forming. If Miss Hadley wished to add to her growing collection of colorful language, she would have been well advised to stay for a moment, he fumed, silently giving vent to a number of words that would have scorched the ears of many of his male friends. He turned abruptly to go in search of some champagne to quench his anger, but after several steps, he paused.

The music had started, the couples were moving in tune with the melody, but something was definitely off key in all of this.

His gaze sought Augusta and her partner for a moment. What the devil was she up to? It suddenly came to him that this was not the first time the gentleman in question had shown her a marked attention. With a slight clenching of his fists he recalled that it was in his arms that she had waltzed the other evening. Why, if he hadn't known her better, he would have thought she was engaging in the sort of behavior most females indulged in when trying to attach the interest of an eligible and attractive gentleman. And perhaps that was a possibility. There was no question that the gentleman was eligible and attractive. However, he was also something else.

He was one of the two names left on her list of suspects.

An involuntary snort escaped his lips. Romantic infatuation indeed! Bloody hell, the chit had some sort of devious scheme planned, he was sure of it! She had already tried housebreaking and thievery. Was abduction and torture next? After all, she had a rather large

footman at her beck and call, so there were a number
of possibilities . . .

The earl found he was suddenly in great need of
that champagne.

As he tossed back a goodly swallow, his thoughts
turned to the heated exchange that had just taken
place. Or perhaps quarrel was a better term for it,
since it had quickly escalated into a nasty war of
words. His breath came out in a sharp sigh. They had
certainly crossed verbal swords in the past, but he had
thought that a truce had been reached some time ago.

In fact, if truth be told, he thought it more than
that. On reflection, he found he would have described
it as an understanding of sorts. While they might not
agree on a number of things, they seemed to have
developed a mutual respect for one another. In a
word, they had become . . . friends.

Or so he had thought.

That made her sharp words even more cutting. She,
of all people, should know that the picture of him
painted by the broad brushes of innuendo was hardly
an accurate portrait of his real self. He drained the
rest of the glass and reached for another as a righteous
anger welled up inside him. It seemed he was sadly
mistaken in thinking she possessed more sense and
intelligence than most people of his acquaintance. So
if she wished him out of her life, he should be happy
to oblige her. He had made every possible effort to
help Edwin Hadley's sister, but if she was too stubborn and too opinionated to accept his help, he should
feel himself well rid of an onerous obligation in the
bargain.

And yet, pride warred with some other emotion as
he set the empty glass down with a thump. Recalling
their former skirmishes, he could picture the fire in
her eyes, so intense that the hazel would be flecked
with amber sparks when she was really stirred to
anger. A ghost of a smile played on his lips. She didn't
hide her feelings very well. It was those expressive

eyes that gave her away. And tonight the look in them had not been that of true anger or indignation, but something infinitely more complex—and vulnerable.

What it was, he couldn't begin to fathom. With a harried sigh, he gave up trying to make sense of it and stalked from the room, muttering darkly under his breath.

Goddamn son of a poxed whore.

Augusta kept a smile pasted on her face, all the while trying to keep her eyes from searching the room for the earl. A surreptitious glance or two revealed that he was still standing in the shadows of the cascading ivy, but his expression was unreadable in the play of light and dark.

"I trust Sheffield was not making himself disagreeable back there." The steps of the dance had brought her and her partner together.

She gave a brittle laugh. "I'm afraid Lord Sheffield and I are usually being disagreeable to each other." After a tiny pause, she added, "It was nothing important. We were merely discussing something about which we could not find a common ground." Out of the corner of her eye, she caught sight of his tall, dark form quitting the room in the direction of the grand staircase.

"Indeed? I cannot imagine why anyone would wish to quarrel with you, Miss Hadley. Pray, what topic could you possibly be arguing over?"

A slight flush came to Augusta's cheeks. "Actually there is precious little on which we don't argue."

His brow once again arched up, but as a perfect gentleman, he forbore to press her further on the matter. A slight smile came to his well-formed lips as he inclined his head a fraction. "Perhaps you would allow me to take you in for supper when this set is finished. I promise I shall endeavor to be more agreeable company than the earl."

"How kind." She dropped her eyes to hide the

gleam of satisfaction that came alight in them. "I should be delighted to sit down with you, Lord Ludlowe. You know, I believe we are neighbors in the country . . ."

The earl turned the page of his morning newspaper with a loud snap. With a peevish snort, he rang for more coffee and waved away the remains of the toast that lay broken into a mound of dry crumbs on his plate. "Cannot Cook manage to turn out a decent slice of bread this morning?"

The footman batted nary a lash as he whisked the offending mess out from under the earl's disgruntled gaze. "Perhaps His Lordship would care for shirred eggs or broiled kippers?"

"Just the coffee, Harding," grumbled Sheffield. "And make sure it is hot." What His Lordship would really care for, he added silently, was a little more sleep and a little less agitated state of mind. How in the devil he had allowed the maddening chit to affect him in such a way was still an utter mystery. It wasn't as if there was any attraction between them—rather the opposite. As she had said, sparks seemed to fly whenever they rubbed together for long. And for whatever the reasons, she did not wish for either his help or his company.

Rather than pacing the floor for a good part of the night, he should have been tossing back a bottle of the finest French brandy to celebrate his good fortune at being freed from the confounded nuisance of worrying about what sort of trouble she would stumble into next. He would do just that, he promised himself. He would join his long-neglected friends this evening and thoroughly douse any lingering thoughts about a certain obstinate, willful, opinionated female.

Sheffield pursed his lips. Hah, that was the problem. Females. One couldn't expect them to be rational. What he really wished for was a chance to share his frustrations and pique—if only on paper—with the one true friend he had. At least Firebrand could be counted on to somehow understand and empathize with his strange mixture of emotions. Damnation, why was the fellow proving so elusive these days?

With a harried sigh, the earl turned his attention back to the printed page, determined to forget about the entire matter. However, the meaning of the endless string of sentences proved as muddled as before. After no more than a minute, he thrust the paper aside and took a gulp of his fresh coffee, nearly burning his mouth on the scalding brew in the process.

An exasperated oath rattled the china. Flinging the heavy damask napkin across the polished mahogany, he rose and stalked from the breakfast room.

A retreat to the library did nothing to improve his mood. He stared balefully at the scribbled notes for another planned speech in Parliament, realizing that before he could continue he needed to consult a certain obscure text in order to verify that his references were correct. As luck would have it, Hatchard's had just that morning answered his urgent request with the news that their only copy had been sold. Perhaps if he sent around to—

Sheffield's head suddenly came up with a jolt. Hell's teeth! He knew he had seen the text recently and now he remembered where.

In Miss Hadley's arms. Right before it had fallen smack into the back of his head.

Once again he was on his feet, threatening to wear a hole through a narrow swath of the expensive Aubusson carpet. After a number of turns, he paused, poker in hand, to stir the banked fire into life. The flames licked up, the logs hissed and crackled, sending off a shower of sparks. The earl watched them fly up, rather like an explosion of fireworks at Vauxhall Gardens.

Sparks be damned! He needed that book. Surely she would not begrudge him the loan of it for a short time, especially since the chances were quite good that

Chapter Ten

Do let me know, dear friend, just what the Red-breasts discover. Much as I am loath to accede to your request to refrain from further action at the moment, I shall respect your wishes. However, if the Beaks prove unable to solve it forthwith, I must insist that you allow me to continue, for I feel that I am on the right track. I shall not burden you with the details, but rest assured that I have fallen onto a most interesting lead. And the sooner this case is solved, the better. I am not the least ashamed to admit how much I miss our intimate—if odd—correspondence. Would that it may begin again soon, my dear friend.

Augusta dropped the note onto her desk, trying hard not to think about the strong, capable fingers that had penned it, fingers that would never again be pressed at the small of her back or twine with hers as the earl twirled her in a graceful arc around the dance floor. Nor did she wish to think about the rest of him—the broad, muscled shoulders, the chiseled jaw, and especially not his eyes. Eyes as deep as any ocean, with currents swirling within them that threatened to drown her in a sea of emotions she had never known existed every time her gaze met his.

She sucked in a lungful of air. This would not do at all. She must no longer think of the earl as a flesh and blood gentleman, but as simply a . . . kindred soul. Her only contact with him from now on was going to be strictly through pen and ink. She took out a fresh sheet of paper to dash off a quick reply to his note, but as another fleeting image of those well-formed lips curled in a rakish smile came to mind, the nib skipped and a spray of droplets marred the letters.

Bloody hell, she swore under her breath, then added a few of the other more descriptive adjectives she had recently learned. This was not going to be easy.

Ignoring the slight tremor in her hand, she finished off the last sentences without further mishap and sealed the letter. Then she unlocked the top drawer of her desk and carefully removed several items wrapped in cloth. A knock on the door nearly caused her to drop the last one as she was placing them in her reticule.

"Miss Augusta, Jamison is waiting out front with the horses." Augusta was relieved to hear the butler's voice rather than that of her mother. "Shall I tell him to take them around to the mews until you are ready?"

"No, no. I am coming." She yanked the drawstring tight and hurried toward the door. But after several steps, she caught herself, turned back and snatched up the missive to the earl. The sooner Jamison delivered it to Pritchard's the better.

The other papers on her desk were ignored, along with the unlocked drawer sitting slightly ajar.

It was early for a morning call, yet Sheffield was too impatient to wait any longer. He had already drawn a number of puzzled looks by driving twice through the park at such an unfashionable hour. No doubt, he thought rather uncharitably, by next week every young sprig would be tooling his phaeton along the Serpentine at some ungodly hour, thinking it all the crack to be doing so.

The earl mounted the marble stairs as his tiger led the team to cool down. The door opened to the sound of the heavy brass knocker and he was ushered inside.

To his chagrin, the elderly butler informed him in a doleful voice that Miss Hadley had gone out.

For a moment, he hesitated. "Have you any idea when she might return?"

The man gave a solemn shake of his head. "Miss Hadley does not always see fit to inform us of her intentions, my lord."

Hah! That he could well believe. His lips tugged downward and the ebony walking stick in his gloved hand began to tap with some force against the side of his well-polished Hessian. It looked as though there was no choice but to try again later—

"Jenkins, I wondered if you might help me with—" Marianne stopped short on catching sight of the earl in the entrance hall.

"I beg your pardon for calling at such an early hour. I was hoping I might find your sister at home," said Sheffield, making a slight bow in her direction. With a cursory glance he took in the softly rounded curves of her petite figure, the halo of golden curls framing her delicate features, and had to admit that if one favored young misses straight from the schoolroom, the girl was indeed a real beauty.

Intimidated by the rather grim scowl on the earl's face, as well as recalling his unflattering assessment of her passed on by Augusta, Marianne's mouth opened and closed several times before any words came forth. "She is . . . out."

"Yes, so I have been informed," he answered dryly.

Marianne colored slightly. "Oh, now you truly think me an idiot, and this time with reason," she blurted out. "I don't usually act as bird-witted as this, but . . . you took me by surprise, sir."

She was not the only one to feel a flush of heat steal to the cheeks. "Forgive me for startling you, Miss Hadley." He cleared his throat. "And it appears I have a good deal more for which to offer apologies, though I must say, it was not terribly diplomatic of your sister to repeat certain unfortunate remarks. I fear I was not in the best of humors that evening and was moved to voice sentiments that were most unfair."

A bit of a twinkle came to Marianne's eyes. "I imagine you have now come to realize that diplomacy is not a trait often associated with my sister."

Sheffield repressed a twitch of his lips. Despite the difference in physical appearance, the family resemblance was quickly becoming obvious. He was indeed wrong to have thought her a vapid milk-and-water miss. It was clear she had at least some of the same sharpness of wit as her sister "Still, she might have done better to hold her tongue."

"Oh, Gus tells me everything." There was a brief pause, after which she added under her breath, "And if she doesn't, I can usually find a way to worm it out of her."

His scowl had by now been replaced by a ghost of a smile. "Did she by chance tell you when she might return?"

"She rode out with Jamison a short while ago, but did not leave any word about when she might be back." A frown came to her face. "Good Lord, she couldn't possibly be trying—" Suddenly aware of what she was saying, her words cut off sharply.

"No, I doubt even your sister would attempt anything really illegal in broad daylight."

Marianne looked a trifle relieved. "I suppose you are right, sir. She may have Jamison twisted around her little finger, but he is not entirely without sense." She paused. "And surely, if she was expecting you—"

The earl gave a slight cough. "As to that, I merely stopped by in the hopes of borrowing a book that I know your sister recently purchased at Hatchard's. It was the last copy, you see."

"Oh." Marianne considered the matter briefly. "Well, I cannot see why she would object to that. If you wish to follow me to her study, I am sure you are welcome to take it with you now—that is, if you can locate it among all the others."

It was clear her sister didn't tell her quite everything, else she would scarcely think that the elder Miss Hadley would find anything about him welcome, least of all his presence. He hesitated a moment, reason warring with curiosity. Perhaps it would be the polite thing to return at a later time, when the lady in question could decide for herself what she wished to do. That such an action would also afford him an opportunity to converse with her was, of course, only of secondary consideration.

However, he had to admit he was intrigued by the idea of seeing her private study, and the sorts of reading material and personal things she surrounded herself with. And after all, he really needed that book. He would have all the more reason to explain his actions to her when he came to return it.

"I should be most grateful," he replied.

"Please follow me then, my lord.'"

He wasn't quite prepared for the sight that met his eyes when Marianne pushed the door open. The desk, nearly as large as his own, was not at all the delicate gilt creation he imagined a young lady would favor. The wide expanse of polished oak was, as Marianne had warned, stacked with a number of weighty volumes, as well as what looked to be a thick manuscript, a large inkwell, and an assortment of pens. Books were also piled on the carpet by her chair and on the settee near the window.

Marianne gave a wry grimace. "I did warn you, sir. Gus is, ah, making a few notes on something that interests her."

"So it would appear."

"Perhaps if you were to tell me the title of what you are looking for I could—"

"Miss Marianne!" Her mother's maid appeared at the doorway, her thin face looking more agitated than normal. "Your mama swears she shall fall into permanent decline if she doesn't locate the special lavender and rosemary vinaigrette she ordered from Gillen and

Trout immediately. She seems to think you might have an idea where it is." The tone was more plea than question.

Marianne bit her lip.

"Do not let me keep you, Miss Hadley."

She looked around uncertainly. "Oh dear, I have no idea where to start. Perhaps it would be best if—"

"I shall just take a quick look around. If I cannot find what I am looking for, I shall come back when your sister is at home."

"You are sure you don't mind?"

"Not at all."

She flashed him a grateful smile. "I shan't be long, my lord."

Sheffield's gaze traveled slowly around the room once the younger Miss Hadley had left. The wallpaper was a pleasant cream and sage stripe, not some flowery confection, its hues picked up by the subtle patterns of the oriental carpet. The simple draperies were pulled back to allow the sunlight to wash over the carved floor-to-ceiling bookcases, each shelf filled to capacity with all manner of leatherbound volumes. Several watercolors hung over the mantel. They were landscapes, showing a bold use of color and unusual technique. They were interesting choices, and ones that revealed a discerning and sophisticated eye.

He turned his attention back to her desk and his mouth quirked upward. A few notes? That appeared to be a vast understatement, though why she was engaged in making such copious jottings was a bit puzzling. However, that was none of his concern, he thought, as he approached the cluttered top. He would just peruse the spines of the books and see if the one he wished to borrow was close at hand.

His fingers ran over the small gold-leafed titles of first one stack, then another. Having no luck, he moved around to the other side of the desk and bent over slightly to check the titles of the third stack. He moved some of the papers aside to have a look at the bottom book and it was then that his gaze fell on a sheet of cream-colored stationery lying among the larger pieces of foolscap. Though folded in half, an edge curled up, just enough to reveal several lines of the handwriting.

His handwriting.

The earl froze in disbelief. After a moment, he gingerly lifted the paper open completely, as if to assure himself he was not hallucinating. But there was no doubt—letter for letter his words stared back at him.

It suddenly felt as if Gentleman Jackson had landed a punishing blow smack in the middle of his chest. Sucking in a deep breath, he sank into the desk chair.

What the devil was his letter to Firebrand doing on Miss Hadley's desk? It made absolutely no sense. None whatsoever. His hand came up to rub at his temple and his eyes fell half closed, barely taking in the other papers lying face-up on the ink-stained blotter. It was some moments before they slowly focused on the distinctive script that covered each sheet, a script that had become nearly as familiar to him as his own hand. In some confusion, his gaze slid to the open drawer, where he spied the rest of his letters, tied in a neat bundle with a length of ribbon.

The awful truth finally hit home.

For a brief second, the room appeared to be spinning. Good Lord, he *was* hallucinating—no, more than that, he was going stark, raving mad! The world was turned totally on its ear, with Miss Hadley writing as a man, and he about to fall away in a dead faint, like some excitable schoolroom miss. That abominable thought helped him get hold of himself.

Then shock started to give way to anger. Why, the nerve of the chit, to attempt such a colossal masquerade as that. To pretend to such wisdom and insight! The oaths that tumbled from his lips would have scorched the ears of even the most grizzled stevedore. Just wait until he got his hands around that slender little neck of hers, he fumed, and then—

The sound of rapid footsteps in the hallway caused his head to jerk up.

"I shall be just a minute. Tell my mother I will be upstairs shortly, as soon as I straighten up some things in my study. Er, what was that, Jenkins?" The brass knob turned with some force and the door was flung open. "You will have to speak up—"

The words cut off abruptly as Augusta caught sight of the earl seated at her desk, the telltale letter still grasped between his fingers.

Her hand came up to her throat as she closed the door behind her. "How dare you, sir!" she said in a strangled whisper. "How dare you break into my private study and paw through my things. Get out! Get out at once!"

"Not until I have some answers from you."

"I have nothing to answer for."

"No?" He rose, as did his voice, and held the piece of paper with his handwriting on it up in the air. "What of this?"

"What of it?" Her eyes dropped to the ground.

"You impudent chit! I cannot believe it! You . . . you tricked me."

"Oh, and how do you figure that? Did I give you false advice? Did I betray your confidences? Did I do anything but . . . act as a true friend?"

He had the grace to color.

"I certainly didn't know either, sir, if that is what you mean," continued Augusta. "Not until very recently." Her eyes were alight with sparks. "Good Lord, you cannot imagine I should ever have written such things if I had any idea it was . . . *you*!"

Sheffield found himself staring at the molten hazel, flecked with amber, and growing hot all over. He took a step closer to her. "Why not?"

"You just answered that yourself, sir. You said you couldn't believe it—you have made it clear that you could never accept that your learned . . . friend was a female."

"Damnation! All the same, you should have told me!"

"Why?" she cried, anger mixing with some other emotion. "What does it matter that *we* don't like each other in the flesh, when something that was of real value to both of us might have been saved?"

The earl took a deep breath. "Is that why you chose to quarrel with me last night?"

Augusta didn't answer, but turned her head to avoid meeting his gaze. He was surprised to see a glimmer of wetness in her eyes. "On top of everything, I suppose you are now going to reveal the true identity of Firebrand and ruin everything I have been working for."

"I should hope you know me better than that," he said in a low voice as he moved even closer.

Her mouth quirked upward in grim humor as she considered his words. "It does appear we know each other very well."

"Hmmm. Very well, indeed." Sheffield was now standing quite close to her and could breath in the faint scent of lavender and lemon from her person.

"Yes, well, er, if you are not going to unmask me, what do you suggest we do about this unfortunate mess?"

"This."

His mouth came down upon hers with an urgency that nearly scorched both of their lips. She struggled to speak but instead of allowing a word, he slipped his tongue deep inside her, twining with hers in a most intimate kiss. All attempt to elude his arms ceased, and with a low cry, she melted against his chest. Tentatively, she began to return his embrace, her fingers stealing up to brush the hard planes of his cheeks.

Her untutored response to him only stoked the fires of his passion. Wild thoughts flamed in his head as his hands pulled her close, molding every soft curve to his body. At that moment, he wanted nothing so much as to strip off all her clothes, lay her glorious body on the carpet before the crackling fire, and make passionate love to her, uniting them physically as one, just as they were joined together in thought.

A groan escaped him as her thumb ran along the line of his jaw. Never before had his self-control gone up in smoke like this. Her simple touch was threatening to burn away every last vestige of the defenses he had carefully constructed around his soul, leaving him naked in his need. Good Lord, in another second he would—

"Lord Sheffield, have you had any luck in—" Marianne's words ended in a squeak of surprise as she clutched at the polished knob to keep the door from swinging open any farther. Eyes widening slightly, she stared in some fascination at the scene before finding her voice again. "Er, well, it seems you are in no need of my help." With that, she pulled the door shut.

Augusta pulled away from Sheffield's chest. "Marianne knew you were here?" she managed to stammer.

"Y-yes. I came here this morning in hopes of borrowing a certain book. She let me in . . . to look for it." His voice sounded equally dazed.

"What book?"

He told her the title.

She moved rather unsteadily to the stack of books by the window and took up the one on top. "Here," she said, hurrying back and thrusting it in his hands. Without waiting for a reply, she continued on in a rush of steps and disappeared into the hallway. Sheffield followed behind her.

They caught up to Marianne in the entrance foyer. "Lord Sheffield has found what he was looking for," announced Augusta in an overloud voice.

Her sister kept her eyes averted from both of them. "Yes, so it seems," she murmured.

Augusta shot her a withering look, then bit her lip.

The earl remained silent as he accepted his curly brimmed beaver hat and walking stick from the elderly butler, who appeared to be staring at his disheveled locks and creased cravat with great interest. Then he cleared his throat with some awkwardness. "I shall return at four to take you out for a drive in the Park."

"I'm afraid that may not be convenient—"

"At four, Miss Hadley." The tone of his voice left little doubt as to whether it was a request or a command.

"Oh, very well."

As soon as the earl was gone, Augusta took her sister by the arm and drew her none too gently into the drawing room. For yet another time that morning, a door was pulled firmly shut.

"I vow, I shall strangle you if you ever mention a word to anyone—including me—about what you witnessed back there," she said through gritted teeth. "It was not as it might have seemed. As usual, we started to argue over, er, a certain matter, and I'm afraid Lord Sheffield had become rather furious with me!"

Marianne arched one delicate brow. "I'm not sure I would have described the earl's emotional state as furious, Gus."

Augusta's face turned a distinct red. "You don't understand how things are between us," she muttered. "Trust me, what was happening back there—"

"It's called kissing, Gus." There was a twinkle in Marianne's eyes. "And it looked like Lord Sheffield was doing it very well indeed."

"If he is very good at it, I imagine it is because he has had a great deal of practice." She let out a ragged sigh. "His kiss did not mean, well, what kisses usually mean. As I was saying, what happened back there had nothing to do with whether the earl feels any attraction for me, but rather with . . ." Her voice trailed off in some confusion.

"Lust?" suggested Marianne.

Augusta tried to appear shocked, but the twitch of her lips gave her away. "Really, Marianne, it's all very well for me, who has no wish to be part of the Marriage Mart, to voice ideas that no proper young miss should be aware of. But you, who have such great prospects, must have a care what you say, even in private, lest you let such words slip out in public."

Marianne's chin jutted out. "As if I should want to be legshackled to a gentleman who would not want to know what I truly think," she said under her breath. Then her expression lightened a bit. "But you are trying to change the subject, and that won't fadge. We were discussing the earl's skill at kissing—"

"We were *not* discussing any such thing," interrupted Augusta. "What I started to say was, Lord Sheffield and I were having a difference of opinion over . . . philosophical ideas. Why, you heard him yourself. He was here to borrow a book."

"Ah, no doubt one from Minerva Press, judging by the sort of debate you two were engaged in."

Augusta's hands set on her hips.

"Oh, very well, I shall stop teasing you. But for someone who is wont to be very observant, Gus, I think you are missing a good deal of what is right before your nose. Literally, that is."

Augusta chose to ignore what her sister might mean by that remark. "I have been trying to keep Lord Sheffield from becoming too involved in my investigation, but"—she paused and pulled a face—"it looks as if I shall be forced to let him do as he pleases, now that he can hold the threat of blackmail over my head."

Marianne frowned. "Because you have written some opinions for Mr. Pritchard?"

"You might say that," muttered Augusta under her breath.

"Well, Lord Sheffield does not strike me as such a narrow-minded gentleman—"

"Hah!"

"—as to think that a female cannot have an independent thought," finished her sister. "Er, how did he know of your writings?"

"Because a certain *someone* saw fit to allow him to enter my *private* study and have free rein among my personal things."

Marianne swallowed hard and looked somewhat abashed. "You cannot deny that he has proven a considerable help so far. I should think you would welcome his help. After all, a short while ago, you were lamenting that the sort of information we needed was most easily obtained by a man. Lord Sheffield most definitely fits that description."

Augusta's eyes narrowed, but her sister kept her features schooled in an expression of great innocence. "Hmmph," she finally said. "I suppose he may prove of some use." Tucking an errant strand of hair behind her ear, she turned a moody gaze upon the blazing fire. "I had better see what it was Mama wanted to see me about. Then, perhaps I might be allowed some peace and quiet to get some work done before I must dress to go driving with the earl."

"Be sure to wear your new sprigged moss-green driving dress, along with the matching chip straw bonnet."

Augusta looked up, utterly nonplussed. *"What?"*

"Naturally you shall want to look your best for the earl, won't you?" With that, Marianne ducked out of the room, before one of the Staffordshire figurines adorning the mantel could come hurtling at her head.

Chapter Eleven

While I, too, miss our exchange of confidences, I must beg of you to respect my wishes, dear friend, and let me settle this affair as I see fit. There are certain aspects about all of this that I prefer to remain private. It is clear from your tone that you are not happy with this decision, however I assure you it is all for the best. I trust it will not be a great deal longer before all of this is behind me, and we may return to our former routine.

The brief letter was tossed onto the desk, along with the earl's York tan driving gloves and the book he had borrowed. Ignoring all of them for the moment, Sheffield made for the sideboard and poured himself a stiff brandy. Though not in the habit of beginning his libations at such an early hour, he decided the events of the past hour merited a glass. Perhaps more than one.

Threading his hand through his dark locks, he took a long swallow, hoping the amber liquid might help dampen his heated emotions. Even now, he was hardly aware of how he had managed to guide his team back through the crowded streets of Mayfair, so reeling had his mind been with the staggering revelation that had taken place in Miss Hadley's study.

It still seemed beyond belief. On more than one occasion during the drive home, he had pressed his eyes firmly shut, hoping that when he opened them again, he might find himself awakened from a terrible dream. Alas, the book under his arm and the lingering taste of the fiery kiss on his lips were all too real. A muttered oath spilled forth from those same lips as the earl sought to make some sense of the strange feelings burning inside him. Anger. Desire. Shock. Longing—he couldn't begin to put a name to it all.

To think that the prickly, opinionated Miss Hadley was, underneath that rather rigid exterior, such a brilliant and original thinker defied imagination. And not only that, her intelligence was not of a dry, ethereal sort, but made infinitely more compelling by her sensitivity and, yes, passion. Sheffield took another hurried gulp of brandy. Passion, indeed! The fiery spirits were not nearly as potent as the memory of her response to his kiss.

After pouring another glass, he took a seat at his desk and took out the packet of her letters from the top drawer where they were safely stowed under lock and key. It was quite some time before he finished rereading each one of them. With a long sigh, he laid them aside, though his eyes could not help from straying back to the flowing script that covered the sheets of crisp ivory paper.

She was right. The perceptiveness and wisdom of their contents were undiminished by the knowledge that their author was a female. Why, if anything, it added a certain allure to the words. The earl steepled his long fingers under his chin and his mouth quirked in a rueful grimace. More than that, it was impossible to deny that a bond had developed that went beyond intellectual matters. Good Lord, they had shared each other's hopes, fears, and weaknesses. And while a part of him might feel angry or deceived, he could not, in all honesty, claim that the relationship had been aught but a source of quiet strength and support to him.

Hell's teeth, it was all so damned confusing! He didn't know quite what he was feeling. His gaze slowly drifted to the banked fire in the hearth. As they lingered on the glowing coals, a realization suddenly flared up within him, as if a match had been set to tinder.

Indeed, he knew damn well what was happening. He simply did not want to admit he was in grave danger, hopelessly, maddeningly in love with the impossible female.

Someone had managed to burn away all the barriers he had carelessly allowed to build up around his true self. It was both frightening and exhilarating—frightening in that he felt so vulnerable, exhilarating in that he no longer had to face the doubts and fears alone. His expression then turned very thoughtful. It was all very well for him to wax romantic over the momentous discovery, but what of Miss Hadley's feelings on the matter? What had she meant when she had said that had she known it was *him*, she never would have said what she did?

His fingers began to drum on the leather blotter. One didn't have to possess an extraordinary intellect to know exactly what she meant.

She might have tender feelings for the author of the letters, but she didn't like *him* above half.

Sheffield drained off the rest of his glass and put it down with a thump. Well, he was simply going to have to convince her that the flesh and blood part of him was just as attractive as his more cerebral attributes. As he recalled the feeling of her every curve molded close to him, the warmth of her lips, the gossamer touch of her fingers on his skin, he felt a surge of heat pooling in his groin. Oh, yes, he most definitely would have to convince her of that.

However, he had no illusions that it was going to be easy. It was important that he not rush his fences, but rather proceed at a more deliberate pace, giving her time to get used to the idea that they might rub along together without creating sparks of the wrong sort. The thought of fireworks brought back to mind their most recent encounter, and her response to his embrace. It seemed there was some cause for hope. After all, she hadn't taken a poker to the side of his head.

The clock on the mantel chimed the hour, reminding him of several obligations that must be seen to before he called once again at Lord Farnum's townhouse. He got slowly to his feet and tucked the bundle of Firebrand's letters carefully back into the desk drawer. So much for ink and paper. It was now time to face the real flame.

As the spirited team of grays slowed to a sedate walk, the two of them eyed each other with a certain wariness. Neither had spoken since the earl had handed Augusta up into his phaeton. Indeed, though nods and greetings had been exchanged with a number of acquaintances also out for a drive at the fashionable hour, neither had so much as glanced in the other's direction. But now, as the vehicle turned onto a quieter path leading to a distant part of the park, an exchange of words seemed unavoidable.

"I suppose I had best apologize—" began Sheffield.

"No doubt you think me—" said Augusta at the same time.

In some embarrassment, they both fell silent. It was the earl who finally spoke up again first. "Er, I would have you know I had no intention of snooping among your things, Miss Hadley. I truly had come to borrow the book, and your sister indicated that I might look for it in your room. That the letter was on your desk was—"

"Was most unfortunate," finished Augusta. She drew in a deep breath. "Still, I was wrong to hurl such accusations at you, sir."

Sheffield cleared his throat. "As to what else took place within the room . . ."

"Please. You needn't mention it." Her cheeks turned a fiery red despite all her resolve to remain cool. "I'm afraid we were both angry and not think-ing clearly."

"Angry?" he repeated faintly.

"Perhaps furious is a better way of putting it," she replied, not meeting his probing gaze. "In any case, could we simply forget that it ever happened?"

Not bloody likely, thought the earl, but if that is what she wished, he would try to act as if it was no great effort to dismiss it as easily as she evidently had done. "Very well, Miss Hadley. It won't be spoken of again."

Augusta breathed an audible sigh of relief. "Good," she said brightly. "Now that we have settled every-thing, you may take me home."

"Oh, we have by no means settled everything. In fact, we have not even begun to discuss the most pressing issues."

The brittle smile disappeared from her face. "What do you mean?" Her voice took on a note of apprehen-sion. "I . . . I thought you said you had no intention of ruining all that I have worked for."

"I don't. Of that you have my promise." He was gratified to see tension in her shoulders relax ever so slightly. "However, there is the serious matter of your investigation."

Her lips pressed together in a tight line. "I was afraid you were going to bring that up."

Sheffield couldn't help but chuckle. "Is it really so odious to contemplate my offer of assistance? Haven't I been of some help?"

Augusta still seemed set on avoiding his eyes. "I do not deny that you have been useful, sir, but as to everything else . . ." She bit her lip. "It is all very confusing. How are we ever going to sort things out?"

Useful, repeated the earl to himself. She might have been speaking about the bootboy or the under foot-man. Good Lord, this was going to prove even more difficult than he imagined.

"Perhaps we might put aside all personal concerns,

as well as our penchant for quarreling, until we have brought whoever is responsible for these terrible deeds to justice."

"You mean, work together?"

He nodded.

She seemed to consider the proposal for an inordinate amount of time. "I suppose the idea does have some merit."

"How kind of you to allow it," replied Sheffield, with a tad more edge than he intended.

Her lips curled upward. "No quarreling, sir. Remember?"

"I doubt you shall let me forget it for a moment." He edged slightly closer to her. "Now, suppose you begin by telling me everything that you have been holding back. And I mean everything."

She stole a quick glance at the earl's diminutive tiger, who was doing his best not to appear fascinated by the most unusual conversation that was taking place. "Ah, perhaps we should wait for some other time."

Sheffield tossed the reins aside. "Henry, take charge of the horses," he called as he jumped down from his perch. "Let us take a stroll among these trees, Miss Hadley. I assure you we will be quite alone, so no more prevaricating." His hands were already around her waist, leaving her precious little room for argument.

They moved off the carriage path and into the shade of the swaying boughs. It was hard to discern her expression in the flickering light, but it appeared that she had decided to go along with his proposal, at least for the present.

"There is really little that you do not already know," she began. As she followed with a more detailed account of all that had happened, it became clear that her words had not been an exaggeration.

The earl ran his fingers along his jaw. "Hmmm. It does seem as if we have narrowed the probable suspects down to two.'' He slanted a sharp glance at Augusta. ''That is, unless you have engaged in some other outrageous exploit that has succeeded in eliminating one of them from consideration?''

''Really, sir!''

He thought he detected a slight deepening of her color. ''Miss Hadley, you haven't answered my question.''

''I haven't done anything,'' she said tartly. ''Under her breath she added, ''At least, not yet.''

''I heard that.''

''Jamison and I were merely having a look at the place,'' she said defensively.

''Absolutely not,'' he growled.

Her eyes took on a certain spark. ''Just because I agreed to allow you to help does not give you the right to lord it over me as if you were—''

''As if I were what? Your brother?'' His head bent closer to hers. ''No, I am most definitely not your brother, but for his sake as well as your own, I intend to see that you don't end up in Newgate. Or Bedlam, for that matter. Surely you can see the sense of coming up with a plan that does not entail foolhardy risks.''

The footpath had taken a turn into a denser copse of trees, and before Augusta had a chance to answer him, two rough looking figures leapt out from the shadows and hurled themselves at the earl. As one of the men knocked her down, Augusta caught the glint of steel.

''They have knives!'' she cried, struggling to regain her feet.

Sheffield was quick enough to parry the first strike. He twisted away to one side, lashing out with his boot to catch his assailant a vicious blow to the knee. With a screech of pain, the man fell to the ground. The second one held back and approached with a bit more caution. The earl slowly backed up, trying to draw both men farther away from Augusta. ''Run,'' he ordered in a low voice. ''Go back to the carriage.''

"I'll not leave you alone!"

"Goddamn son of a poxed—" Sheffield's words cut off as the first man recovered his footing and made another lunge at his midriff. This time, he knocked the man's arm up with one forearm, then delivered a hard jab to the fellow's ribs, drawing a torrent of foul curses.

"Watch your bloody language," snapped the earl as he landed another punch. "There is a lady present."

While Sheffield was engaged in fighting off one attack, the second assailant had edged around to come at him from the rear.

"Behind you, sir!" warned Augusta, throwing herself forward.

Sheffield tried to dodge away, but the fellow managed to get a firm hold of his arms. The first attacker's blade slashed out, but at the last moment it fell short as his head snapped back from the impact of a flying reticule. The man staggered back, dazed, the knife falling from his grasp. His comrade, on seeing what had happened, let go of the earl and took to his heels. The other man, his wits fast recovered, decided to do the same.

Sheffield drew in a deep breath and regarded the wicked looking slash through his clothing.

"Good heavens, are you alright, my lord?" cried Augusta, running up to take hold of his arm.

His head came up, a wry expression on his face. "Ah, another waistcoat slain, I'm afraid."

"It's nothing to joke about. You might have been killed!" Her fingers came out to touch his side. "Why, you're hurt!" she cried in a stricken voice, staring at the trace of blood on her glove.

"Hardly a scratch," he said lightly. "They were certainly very desperate footpads, to risk accosting law-abiding citizens in broad daylight."

Her mouth compressed in a grim line. "I should hope you wouldn't think me so addlepated as that, sir.

You know as well as I those were no thieves in search of a plump purse. They meant to do you harm."

"Yes," he agreed. "They did. How perceptive of you, Miss Hadley." The irritation in his voice was becoming more pronounced with each word. "So why, may I ask, did you not obey my order and take yourself off to safety when you had a chance?"

She fixed him with a withering look. "Oh, that would have been a fine thing to do, leaving you alone to face two of them by yourself. Did it occur to you that a female might possess a sense of honor as well as a brain? Besides, we just agreed we are working together. Remember?"

He muttered something under his breath.

"And instead of raking me over the coals for it, you should be thanking the fact that I didn't fall into a fit of vapors, else your so-called scratch might have been considerably worse."

"What the devil was in that reticule?" he demanded, walking rather gingerly to where it lay among the leaves.

"Oh, a brass spy glass, a tape measure, and a set of picklocks." On catching sight of the expression that came to his face, she hastened to add, "I told you, we were just having a look." Then she gave an injured sniff. "You *could* say thank you."

He returned to her side. "I could also do a number of other things, but being a gentleman, I shall restrain the urge to throttle you."

She opened her mouth to retort but stopped abruptly on seeing the look in his eyes.

"However," he continued in a soft voice, "you are right. Thank you."

"You . . . you are quite welcome, my lord."

Sheffield's hand brushed hers as he looped the strings of the reticule over her wrist.

Augusta gave a tiny shiver and her head ducked down, hiding her face. "Falling coping stones, murderous cutthroats—I see that for your sake as well as that

of the children, we shall have to put our heads together and solve this as soon as possible."

"Not to speak of my wardrobe," he added dryly.
"Though no doubt Weston will be delighted to—" His
words cut off in mid-sentence and his hand came up
to smack his forehead. "Good Lord, how stupid of
me! Why didn't I think of it before?"

"*What?*"

"Waistcoats!"

"Really, sir, I am aware of your sartorial reputation,
but I hardly think the matter of your torn waistcoat
is of primary importance at the moment."

"Not *my* torn waistcoat. Come, Miss Hadley, I expect sharper thinking from you."

Augusta's brow creased. "You mean, the scrap of
silk I found at the scene of the crime?"

"Precisely."

"I still fail to see the connection."

"You just voiced it a moment ago," he replied. "As
I am a leader of fashion, most any tailor would jump
through hoops to have my business. I have only to
show a bit of material that has caught my fancy and
ask if the man has it—"

"—and who else he has made such a garment for,"
finished Augusta. A brilliant smile spread over her
face. "That's very clever, my lord. It seems I was correct in thinking you would be of some use."

Sheffield took a firm grip of her elbow. "Aren't I
just," he muttered through gritted teeth. "Perhaps I
might also make myself useful by conveying you
home. It is getting late."

They began walking back toward the earl's waiting
phaeton. Augusta slanted a glance at the scowl dark-
ening his face and slowed her steps. "Are you by
chance angry about something, my lord?"

"Angry? Why, quite the contrary, Miss Hadley."
The sarcasm in his voice couldn't have been thicker
had he mixed it with linseed oil. "I am in alt on being

deemed useful. Think of all the marvelous things that are considered useful—a dog, a walking stick, a—"

"Oh dear, I've hurt your feelings."

"I've more real injuries to worry about than a blow to my pride," he growled, wincing slightly as his boot slipped on a loose stone.

She came to a complete stop. "Forgive me, sir," she said softly. "With all the talk of ruffians and fabrics, I'd quite forgotten about your wound."

"Really, it's naught but a—*ouch!* What are you doing?"

Augusta continued to work at the buttons of his waistcoat. "Stop squirming. I am taking a look at your . . . ribs." She swallowed hard as her hand parted the fine linen of his shirt and revealed a goodly amount of flesh.

Sheffield did, indeed, cease any sort of movement.

The tips of her fingers started to trace along the thin red line made by the knife. "It does not look overly serious, but you must make sure to put some basilicum powder on it and have it bandaged properly," she said after a moment, trying hard not to stare at the chiseled muscles of his abdomen. Then, letting the shirt fall closed, she straightened and made a show of adjusting the hem of her glove. "You are very lucky, my lord. Another inch and you might have been . . . killed." Suddenly, tears seemed to spring from nowhere.

The earl reached out to pull her close. "No need to upset yourself. I assure you, I have no intention of cocking up my toes any time in the near future." A gentle humor stole into his voice. "At least not until I have finished being useful to you in this matter."

Augusta, her face buried against the soft wool of his jacket, made a sound somewhere between a laugh and a sob. "I don't usually behave in such a silly, missish fashion."

He gave a chuckle. "I daresay you've experienced enough shocks today to throw even Boadicea into a fit

of vapors." His hand stroked lightly over her shoulder.
"You know, you were quite as magnificent as the War-
rior Queen herself, attacking that ruffian with the
knife." There was a slight pause. "However, if you
ever do anything that foolhardy again, I shall forget I
am not your brother and take you over my knee."

"My Lord!" Her head jerked up, the tears gone,
replaced by a martial light in her hazel eyes. "If you
think—"

"Augusta."

The rest of the words caught in her throat.

"Considering all we have been through together, I
think it might be appropriate that we call each other
by our Christian names. Mine is Alexander, in case
you have forgotten."

She stood absolutely still, save for the flutter of a
pulse at her neck.

"Actually, I think I prefer Gus," he went on. "That
way, I can delude myself into thinking I am still speaking to a male friend."

There was a slight waver to her voice when she
finally spoke. "Are you so very disappointed that I
am not . . . a man?"

"Hmmm. Well, on second thought, the fact of your
being female adds some rather interesting facets to
the relationship." His head dropped a touch lower,
placing his lips quite close to hers.

"My lord," she stammered.

"Alex," he corrected. The progress of his mouth
toward hers was arrested by the sound of rapid
footsteps.

"Guv!" The little tiger skittered to a halt on seeing
the earl with Augusta in his arms. "I seen two werry
seedy lookin' coves scarper from here, and when ye
didn't appear soon arfter, I thought I best see if ye
was alwright." He kicked at the dirt. "But I sees ye
ain't in need of any assistance."

Sheffield repressed an oath, along with his simmering desire. "Sharp eyes you have, Henry," he said

Chapter Twelve

I trust the day's activities have not proven too strenuous for you to put in an appearance at the Grenvilles' ball tonight. Knowing you as I do, I cannot think that such a paltry event as having your life put at risk would have the least effect of dampening your spirit—at least I hope that your nerves are stronger than that, for I need that scrap of waistcoat if I am to begin my inquiries first thing in the morning.

It had been rather strange to read the earl's words, knowing that, for the first time they were truly addressed to her and not some phantom being no more substantial than a scribble of ink on paper. Augusta gave an inward sigh on once again considering their meaning. While it was clear he did not expect her to fall into a girlish fit of megrims, she was not quite sure whether to be heartened or discouraged by that fact. Or the fact that he preferred to call her Gus. No matter that those who knew her best did so too. With him, it was—how had he put it?—so that he might delude himself into imagining his friend was still a man.

Her mouth tugged into a slight grimace. She had best not delude herself into imagining that Sheffield saw her as anything but a feisty bluestocking who hurled argumentative words and reticules with equal abandon. And it really was no use thinking that might change. She had precious little of the delicate sensibili-

ties a man desired in a female. He might prove broad-
minded enough to tolerate her oddities without overt
disgust, but more than that—

"Gus, have you heard a word I have been saying?"

She gave a guilty start and forced her eyes to stop
searching the crowded ballroom. "Forgive me, Jamie.
I fear my thoughts had momentarily strayed else-
where."

"To China, by the look of it," murmured Ashford.
"Is something the matter? You have been acting
rather odd recently."

Odd. There it was again. Even her oldest friend
thought her strange. "I have been distracted by certain
concerns," she answered vaguely, brushing at the folds
of her gown to mask her unsettled feelings.

He shot her a quizzical glance, then all at once a
slow smile started to spread across his face. "Does it
perchance have anything to do with the attentions of
a certain gentleman?"

Much to her chagrin, Augusta's face turned a decided shade of red.

Ashford's expression turned into a sly grin. "I
thought I had noticed that Ludlowe was taking a
marked interest in you," he said with a note of satisfaction at being so observant. "He seems a fine
enough fellow, and now that I think on it, it makes a
good deal of sense that he is on the lookout for a
suitable bride, what with the prospect of soon coming
into his uncle's title." Before Augusta could find her
tongue to disabuse him of such a corkbrained notion,
he gave her a little wink and continued on. "Never
doubted you would catch on, especially now that you
have chosen to, er, dress a little differently than your
usual style."

He took her utter silence as confirmation of his
hunch. "Well, I don't blame you for being distracted.
When one's thoughts are riveted on . . ." He began
to wax poetic about the object of his own affections,
giving Augusta a moment to recover.

"Forgive me, but I must be off to find Cynthia. Do you wish to remain seated here or—"

"Yes, I shall be fine," she answered quickly, her mind already mulling over what he had brought up. Her initial urge to dismiss his conjectures as absurd gave way as she thought about it, and a speculative gleam came to her eyes. It was true that she had encouraged Ludlowe's attentions on several occasions, hoping to pump some sort of useful information out of him. After all, his was one of the two names left on her list. But so far their conversations had not progressed much past the normal sort of pleasantries.

However, if she were to give the impression that her feelings were more than simply neighborly, she might be able to learn something of value in some intimate, unguarded moment. Her eyes pressed closed. Could she pull it off? Could she bat her eyelashes or simper convincingly enough to make him think she had developed a *tendre* for him? And would it do any good? Her brow furrowed slightly. If rumors were at all true, Ludlowe needed a rich wife, so perhaps she wouldn't need to depend on mere charm to fix his attention. After all, it was not a secret that she would come into a marriage with a sizeable dowry.

"I would ask what has brought such a grim expression to your face, but I fear I wouldn't want to know." So intent was Augusta on working out her plans that she had failed to notice Sheffield's approach. His mouth twitched as a guilty look flashed over her features. "Ah, I see that I am not far off the mark."

"You are not the only one thinking of how to discover the information we need," she said under her breath, turning to watch the musicians warming up in prelude to a new melody in hopes of hiding the stain of color that once again was rising to her cheeks. Drat the man, she thought rather irritably. And drat herself! Was the simple sound of his voice going to cause a heat to course through her every time they met?

Sheffield chuckled. "That's exactly what I was afraid

of." His hand came around her elbow. "Come, let us find some refreshment." In a lower voice he added, "There appears to be a quiet spot in the corner where we might continue this discussion with a modicum of privacy."

Augusta let him lead her away from the crowd and fetch her a glass of ratafia punch. "You don't imagine that I mean simply to hand over the only hard bit of evidence and go back to my embroidery, do you?" she said rather acidly as he passed her a glass.

"You embroider?" He took a long swallow of his champagne. "I would not have imagined it possible."

"Oh, you know what I meant."

"Unfortunately I do."

"Lord Sheffield," she began.

"Alex," he corrected in soft voice. "Remember?"

Her mouth suddenly felt very dry. "Very well . . . Alex. It's just that I . . . you see, I, too, have a plan. Of sorts. That is . . ." Why was it that she couldn't seem to manage a coherent sentence?

The earl appeared to ignore her stammerings. "Did you bring the piece of waistcoat?"

"Of course I did." She fumbled with her reticle and withdrew the scrap of silk.

He slipped it into his pocket. "Now, you may as well tell me what plan you have been cultivating in that fertile mind of yours. I daresay I shall learn about it soon enough."

Augusta drew her chin up a fraction higher.

"Gus," he warned. "I thought we had a deal. If we are to work together, we must keep each other informed as to our intentions."

The trouble was, she thought with wry dismay, she hadn't realized the deal would include having her pulse start to race out of control whenever he was near her. Her fingers tightened around her glass as the faint scent of bay rum wafted from his freshly shaven cheek. Daring a quick glance in that direction, she found herself fighting the urge to run her hand over the tanned skin, to twine it in the long, dark locks curling around his ear. Appalled at where her thoughts were headed, as well as the fact that they might be transparent, she forced her gaze out to where the couples were swirling by in a blur of color.

The earl gave a bemused smile. "Is it that bad?"

Had he really guessed even the half of it? She sucked in her breath. "Is what so bad?" she asked faintly.

"Your plan, of course." He regarded the contents of her glass with an arch of his brow. "Has someone dumped a bottle of blue ruin in the punch, for you are beginning to act a trifle bosky."

"Don't be ridiculous," she muttered, secretly relieved it was that to which he had been referring. "I am in complete control of my senses."

"That might be a matter of some debate, but enough of this verbal fencing, Gus. Out with it."

"It is nothing to make such a fuss over. I merely intend to see if I might encourage Lord Ludlowe's attentions . . ."

Sheffield's expression turned very grim.

". . . and manage to coax some slip of the tongue from him."

"And just how, may I ask, do you intend to coax a slip of the tongue?" he asked in a very deliberate voice.

"Well, er, in the usual way that females do such things."

There was a moment of ominous silence before the earl's jaw unclenched enough for him to speak. "Absolutely, unequivocally not."

"You have no right to order—"

"Are you stark, raving mad?" he continued, ignoring her feeble protest. "Have you conveniently forgotten that, if your suspicion is at all right, this is a very dangerous man? You saw just this afternoon what he is capable of if he thinks his plans are in the least threatened."

"I shall be careful, of course."

"Of course," he mimicked. "And of course, since the brilliant Miss Hadley is infinitely more clever than any mere male, there is no chance of any mishap along the way."

Augusta's hands balled into fists at her side. "Odious, overbearing man," she retorted in a near whisper.

"Stubborn, willful termagant," he replied through gritted teeth.

There was a discreet cough as a well-dressed figure paused in his approach. "I had hoped to claim my spot on your card, Miss Hadley, but if you would rather continue what looks to be a fascinating conversation, I could return at another time." Ludlowe's cool gaze regarded the two faces before him, each rigid with anger, and a look of faint amusement played on his lips.

"Indeed not," said Augusta emphatically, reaching out her hand to him with what she hoped was a brilliant smile. "I am delighted at the prospect of having the chance to enjoy such a charming partner as you, sir." Her tone left little doubt as to her opinion of her present company.

Ludlowe gave a slight bow, then proffered his arm. "Well then, if you will excuse us, Sheffield, I believe the set is forming."

It was only with great difficulty that the earl restrained the urge to utter a certain oath aloud. But he thought it as he watched Augusta walk away arm in arm with the other man. Hell's teeth! he added for good measure. Didn't she have any idea of how perilous a course she might be setting for herself? After a moment's consideration, he decided the problem was not that she failed to grasp the danger, but rather that she refused to allow it to stop her.

His foot began to tap impatiently on the polished parquet. No doubt she would take great pains to avoid being alone with him any time during the rest of the evening. He could hardly pick her up and bodily carry her from the room, though the thought was sorely tempting—for more than one reason. Why was it that even when he was furious with her, those flashing hazel eyes had the most unsettling physical effect on his person? As she had brushed past him, he had wanted to reach out and stop her, not the least because his fingers were burning to feel the soft heat of her cheek and bury themselves once more in the silken splendor of those wheaten tresses.

With a start, Sheffield realized it was a waltz that was playing, and that she and her partner were gliding toward where he stood. His eyes locked on the gentle swaying of her hips, then moved up to the gloved hand lightly pressed at the small of her back. For an instant it was he, too, and not just an unknown villain, who was contemplating murder. Then, getting a grip on his emotions, he turned on his heel and stalked to the far end of the room where he sought another glass of champagne to dampen down the worst of his ire.

"Good evening, Lord Sheffield."

The earl's head jerked around. He had come to a halt next to where Marianne, not yet approved by the patrons of Almack's to waltz, and one of her admirers were sitting out the dance. Wiping the scowl off his face as best he could, he gave a curt nod in acknowledgment of her greeting. "Good evening, Miss Hadley. I trust you are enjoying the activities as much as your sister is." The words came out rather more sharply than he had intended.

Marianne's eyes stole a quick glance at Augusta turning in step with Lord Ludlowe and a slight crease furrowed her smooth brow. It disappeared in an instant, replaced by her usual sunny expression. "Yes, the music is quite delightful. Indeed, I find I have worked up quite a thirst on the dance floor." Turning to her partner with a charming smile, she said, "Lucas, would you mind terribly fetching me a glass of lemonade? And perhaps another glass of champagne for His Lordship?"

The young man by her side jumped to his feet with alacrity. "Of course, Miss Marianne."

As soon as he had hurried off, she spoke again, concern replacing gaiety in her voice. "Has something changed that Augusta has not seen fit to mention to me, sir, or is Lord Ludlowe still among the prime suspects?"

The earl slanted her a look of grudging approval for such a quick grasp of the matter even as his mouth set in a grim line. "You are not mistaken. Once again, your sister has seen fit to throw caution to the wind and sail full tilt into battle. But this time I fear she is facing the very real risk of running hard aground." He drew in a breath. "She means to encourage some measure of intimacy between them, with the idea of wheedling the incriminating evidence out of him. If Ludlowe is the guilty party, he has proven that he is no fool. Nor is he a man to be trifled with, as the events of this past afternoon have proved."

Marianne went a bit paler. "What do you mean, sir?"

"She did not tell you of the attack?"

"No. She did not."

His lips compressed even more. "As you see, she does not see fit to tell you everything."

Marianne drew in a ragged breath. "Is there nothing you can do to convince her to abandon such a perilous course? She seems to . . . pay some attention to you."

A muttered "Hah!" was the only reply. He then lapsed into a gloomy silence and appeared to be contemplating the tips of his polished Hessians. After several minutes, he cleared his throat and was about to speak again when interrupted by the reappearance of Marianne's admirer.

"Here is your lemonade, Miss Marianne." Lord Andover's cheerful tone faltered on taking in the stony expressions that met his words. "And, er, your champagne, sir."

"I believe Miss Hadley requested ratafia punch. The champagne you may leave with me."

The young man handed the glass over to the earl. "But Alex, she most definitely said—"

"Are you contradicting the lady?" inquired Sheffield softly. "Or me?"

"Ah, no, sir."

"Good. Especially if you expect me to stand you for the Four-in-Hand Club any time soon."

Without further argument, the young man headed off into the milling crowd with even more haste than the first time.

Marianne observed the interchange between the two men with some interest. "You appear to have some acquaintance with Lord Andover, sir. He, ah, seems to defer to your wishes without question."

"Unlike a certain someone else," growled the earl under his breath. "But yes, Lucas is quite used to my barking orders at him. I've been doing it since he was in leading strings." At her look of puzzlement, he added, "He is my cousin."

"Oh, I did not know that. How . . . interesting." She fiddled with the strings of her reticule. "You were about to say something, my lord, before he appeared?"

Sheffield pursed his lips. "I have a suggestion that may help to protect your sister from harm, but it involves a bit of, shall we say, subterfuge on your part. I need not add that she would not be best pleased were she to discover your hand in it."

"I should be grateful for any idea you have. Please tell me what you have in mind." Her jaw set. "Gus is not the only one capable of action."

The earl repressed a twitch of his lips. "So it seems," he murmured. "Well, I believe there is little likelihood that Ludlowe would attempt anything rash during such a gathering as this. However, an invitation for a drive in the park, an excursion to Vauxhall—these would all be cause for concern. If you were to, ah, keep abreast of your sister's plans, you could contrive to send word to me of these sorts of things."

"You mean spy on her?"

"If it comes to that, yes." He paused. "It is a pity we cannot keep her under lock and key, but at the very least we can make sure she is kept under a watchful eye. That is, if I can count on your aid. I do not like to ask you to betray any confidences, but in truth, I can think of nothing else."

She nodded in understanding. "I think it an excellent plan. You may depend on me, sir."

The earl gave a faint smile. "I'm sure I can, Miss Hadley. Now, do you think that big footman of hers might be enlisted to be part of our plan?"

"Jamison? Oh, I think we'll have little trouble convincing him it is for the best," She thought for a moment. "But what of during the night. She has been known to, er, slip out at odd hours."

"Yes, so I have noticed." He rubbed at his chin. "I know of a man who will serve our purpose there. Trust me, your sister will not escape unnoticed the next time she takes it into her head to embark on some nocturnal sojourn. In the meantime, of course, I shall be doing my best to resolve this whole matter with my own inquiries."

"The waistcoat?"

He nodded.

"Oh, I do hope you shall discover who the culprit is soon and put an end to his awful deeds."

"Learning his true identity is one thing, proving it to the authorities is quite another, Miss Hadley. It won't be easy, but I mean to see that justice will prevail in the end, no matter what it takes."

On that grim note, the dance came to an end and the earl saw his earlier suspicions were not unfounded. Augusta made a point of being escorted back to where several of her mother's acquaintances were seated together exchanging the latest on-dits. Taking a chair at the edge of the little group, she leaned forward slightly, as if intent on catching their every word. Sheffield's eyes narrowed, knowing full well that the gesture was prompted more out of a desire to avoid any look from him than from any interest in what was being said.

He tossed back the remainder of his drink and handed the empty glass to a passing footman. "Since it appears unlikely that I shall have any further chance of talking some sense into your sister, I believe I shall excuse myself, Miss Hadley." He gave a slight bow in her direction. "For the next little while, there will always be a young urchin in the square across from your townhouse—you have only to send one of your footmen with a note and it will reach me at any time of the day or night."

As he walked away, he noticed Andover turn from where he had been studying a towering arrangement of potted flowers and venture back to the young lady's side, ratafia punch in hand. The young man had some sense, he noted with satisfaction. Lucas had always been his favorite cousin and it pleased him that the pup was showing both a laudable tact in his actions and commendable taste in his choice of females. And at least his relative was making some headway with his suit, judging by the smile that came to the younger Miss Hadley's face.

The same could hardly be said for himself.

He couldn't help but steal another glance at Augusta. Just as he suspected, her attention was anything but riveted on the conversation taking place among the ladies. Her expression was scrunched into the peculiar look he had come to recognize as meaning some truly devious thoughts were being formed inside that lovely head of hers. He knew the best course of action was to take himself off, but as her eyes caught his, then turned quickly away, he abruptly changed his mind. Veering across the room, his steps brought him to a halt in front of her chair.

"Hmmmm. Let me see, I believe I am penciled in for the next dance." He reached down for her card before she could snatch it away, and made a show of examining it while surreptitiously scribbling something in the empty space. "Yes," he announced in a loud voice. "So I am."

Three turbaned heads swiveled around to observe them with great interest.

Augusta's jaw clenched on realizing she had been outmaneuvered, but as there was little she could do, short of creating a scene, she reluctantly rose and allowed the earl to take her arm.

"That was an underhanded trick," she said under her breath.

"Rather the pot calling the kettle black when it comes to being devious, my dear."

She flushed, more at the endearment than the accusation.

"Besides, the tabbies looked as if they could do with something else to talk about. Oh, by the way, what was the topic of such a spirited discussion?"

"Ahhh . . ." Her color deepened, causing him to chuckle. "I warn you, I refuse to be drawn into further argument with you on the subject," she continued rather tartly.

"I have no intention of brangling anymore tonight," he replied mildly, his head bent close to her ear.

She swallowed hard. "What . . . what are your intentions, then?"

"Why, to dance, Gus."

His hand took hold of hers and though the figures did not allow quite the same intimacy as a waltz, Sheffield felt a surge of heat in his groin. The light touch of her fingers, the faint scent of her perfume, the brush of her gown at his thighs—his eyes pressed closed for a moment as he savored the very nearness of her. Then he regarded her rigid features. Good Lord, was she really so unmoved by what had happened that morning in her study? Why, like some randy schoolboy, he could hardly stop thinking of the taste of her mouth, the texture of her tresses, the softness of her breasts, yet here she was, by all appearances according the event no importance at all.

He found himself nearly bungling a simple step. Did their encounter really mean so little to her? Another quick glance showed only an expression shuttered to any probing looks. At the time, he had thought her not entirely adverse to his heated kisses. In fact, she had seemed to return them with a certain spark of her own. But now? He held back a sigh. Earlier in the day, she had snapped an angry retort to the effect that had she known he was Tinder, she never would have revealed so much of herself. Was it such a sad disappointment, then, for her to learn that her intimate friend was . . . himself?

The thought was not at all a pleasant one.

"Sir." There was a brief pause. "Alex."

His head jerked around.

"The music has stopped," she said in a low voice.

"Hmmmph. So it has."

That drew a ghost of a smile from her. "Engrossed in thinking of ways to do bodily harm to me?" she inquired lightly.

Sheffield drew in a breath. Her body had most definitely been figuring in his thoughts, but hardly as she imagined. Forcing a semblance of a smile, he made a noncommittal sound in his throat as he led her from the floor.

Her brows drew together for an instant on taking in his enigmatic expression, then she suddenly changed the subject. "You were engaged in a long conversation with my sister." There was a hint of question in the terse statement.

Ah. So she had not been entirely unaware of his movements. "Yes, a quite enjoyable one," he replied, and his smile became genuine. "Allow me to apologize again for my earlier foolish comments. You were entirely right to ring a peal over my head. She is a most interesting young lady—charming, perceptive, intelligent." To his surprise, he felt her hand stiffen on his arm.

"Yes, she is a very special person."

The earl thought he detected a note of brittleness in her voice. Puzzled, he gave up any designs of leading her toward the garden. Her mood seemed as unsettled as his own, and rather than risk further fireworks, he turned their steps back in the direction of the cluster of tabbies.

"Thank you for the dance," he murmured politely, bowing over her hand. "Good evening, Miss Hadley." Without waiting for a reply, he gave a rakish smile to the three ladies and strolled away.

Augusta swallowed hard, trying to dislodge the lump in her throat. So the earl found her sister . . . interesting. It was hardly surprising, she told herself. Still, she couldn't help but feel a tiny stab of jealousy knife through her on recalling his dark head bent close to Marianne's in earnest conversation. An instant later she was ashamed of such a base emotion, but contrition did little to improve her depressed spirits. If only she had a crumb of Marianne's easy manner with gentlemen. She blinked back the sting of a tear. Well, it was no use wishing for the moon. The only thing she did have to recommend herself was her brain, so she might as well concentrate her efforts on putting it to some use.

With that, she forced her thoughts away from Sheffield and back to the formidable task of how to trap a dastardly villain.

Chapter Thirteen

Well? You've had over a day. What have you discovered?

Sheffield had to repress a bark of reluctant laughter at how changed in tone her correspondence had become. No more warm greetings, no more exchange of opinions or feelings.

Just business.

Picking up his pen to reply, he couldn't help but wonder on it. Why did she insist on treating him with such coolness? If she liked him on paper, why could she not show at least some regard for him in person? All vanity aside, he was not unaware of how most females reacted to him. Surely she did not find him objectionable to look at, so it must be something else. What that was, he couldn't quite figure out.

He toyed with the bottle of ink, recalling a number of her written musings. Though he hadn't really thought about it overly, it seemed she was wont to dwell on how she didn't fit into Society, how estranged she was from the superficial gaiety and charm. And more than once in his presence, she had let slip a comment about her lack of physical endowments. Was that really how she saw herself—an unattractive, awkward female with no redeeming qualities?

An exasperated sigh sounded from his lips. It couldn't be. She was too intelligent not to realize that her unique intellect, coupled with her intriguing looks, made her . . . irresistible. So there had to be another, more plausible reason, but damned if he could fathom what it was. Giving up for the moment, he scrawled off a brief note and rang for a footman.

Despite the fact that she persisted in calling him odious and insufferable, he couldn't ignore the temptation to see her again. If she wanted information, she would have to consent to a drive.

Augusta dropped the paper into her lap, a scowl creasing her face. Drat the man! Why couldn't he just write what he had to say? Or did he enjoy teasing the color to her face? Even now she could feel a faint heat come to her cheeks on thinking of him. His physical presence ignited a more telling reaction. But duty called, she reminded herself. She needed to know what he had learned and so she would have to endure his company, no matter how difficult it was on her senses.

She took up her pen and dashed off a reply with enough force on the nib to send a fine spray of droplets spattering across the paper.

Promptly at four, a knock on the door heralded the earl's arrival. He was nothing if not punctual, she thought grimly as she tied the ribbons of her bonnet snugly under her chin. Then, like a knight settling his helm in place for battle, she gave it one last tug and set off, ready to begin their jousting.

Sheffield seemed unperturbed by her deliberate silence. In fact, he appeared to be whistling under his breath as they turned into the park. Augusta had expected a clash of verbal swords rather than this nonchalant display of good humor. Rattled, she dropped her own pose of disinterested detachment.

"Well?"

He slanted a sideways look at her. "A fine afternoon for a drive, is it not, Gus?"

"The weather has been uncommonly nice for this time of year, the price of kid gloves has become exorbitant, the neckline of the gown Lady Fitzwilliam wore last week was shocking, and the latest offering at Haymarket Theatre is said to be quite entertaining. There, we have dispensed with all the rest of the prattle, so now can we get down to business?"

The earl chuckled. "You forgot one thing." His eyes ran over the navy merino carriage dress and snug little jacket frogged in military fashion that Marianne had chosen for her. "You are looking very well, Gus."

She ducked her head, hoping to hide her blush. Good Lord, it was difficult enough sitting close beside him and pretending to be unmoved without having to listen to such pleasant banter. Teeth on edge, she forced a cool reply. "I believe you have something of greater importance to tell me, sir."

"Alex," he corrected. "I thought we had come to an agreement on that."

"Well, have you?"

"Have I what?"

"Something to tell me!" she snapped with some impatience.

His brow rose slightly.

"Alex," she added in a near whisper.

His lips twitched. "As a matter of fact, I have." The horses slowed to a sedate trot. "Weston and Stutz have never seen the fabric. Nor have any of the other tailors on Bond Street or Jermyn Street."

"Oh, that's helpful," she remarked rather snidely.

He shot her an aggrieved look before continuing. "I didn't say that was all, did I? There are others, of course, in less fashionable locations that are not as well-known, but more willing to offer a gentleman generous terms in return for his patronage." He paused to grimace. "You have no idea how many ghastly waistcoats and ridiculous chitterlings I have been forced to view."

"A sore trial, I am sure."

"Just so. Now, neither Gibbons nor Thurgood nor Haskins had the silk. Then I remembered Joshua Hallinsworth near Regent's Park . . ."

She began to grind her teeth.

". . . but alas, no luck there. Although, oddly enough, I did find a rather attractive paisley pattern in dark burgundy and navy that—"

"Alex!"

"You do not care for paisley?"

"If you say another word about a color or pattern other than the one which we are seeking, I will finish the job those two ruffians set out to do myself!"

"Don't tell me you have added a knife to the gruesome assortment of weapons in that reticule of yours." Before she could snap a retort, he ceased his teasing. "But if you insist, we'll dispense with your opinion on sartorial splendor. What you wish to hear is the name Shackleford."

Augusta looked thoroughly perplexed.

"I wouldn't have thought of his name either. Not my taste at all. But the dreadful fellow was so anxious to curry my favor that he dug around in his workshop until he emerged victorious with several yards of the silk."

"*Our* silk?"

"The same. And a rare one at that. Apparently only one bolt survived a leaky hull and long passage from China. He bought it, along with several other remnants, from the shipper at a favorable price."

"So we may assume that not many garments have been made from the stuff," she said very slowly.

"I think it is safe to say so."

"And this Shackleford, he remembers his clientele?"

"He does, though hastening his recall cost me the order of a garment I shall relegate to the wastebin as quickly as possible."

"Please stop teasing," she urged. "What did he tell you?"

The earl took a moment to guide his team around a sharp bend, then brought the phaeton to a complete stop in the midst of a copse of elm and hawthorne. "Ludlowe is our man," he said softly.

"Oh, now we know for certain who is the miscreant behind these terrible crimes." She leaned toward him with a radiant smile and placed a hand on his arm. "Alex, how very clever of you!"

"I've proven useful, haven't I?"

There was something about his tone that caused her expression to turn wary. "Yes, indeed you have," she answered rather hesitantly.

"Then perhaps I should be rewarded for my efforts."

Augusta couldn't quite believe her ears. Her mouth dropped open, but for a moment she was unable to speak. "Shame on you, sir," she finally managed to sputter. "I had not thought you so mercenary as to expect a sum—"

"It's not money I'm speaking of, Gus."

She bit at her lower lip. "J-just what did you have in mind?"

There was no answer as he dropped the reins and bent his head toward hers. This time the kiss was softer, gentler, his lips merely grazing over hers at first. She recoiled as if burned, but his hands had come up around her shoulders and stopped her from pulling away. "Am I truly that odious?" he murmured before taking possession of her mouth again.

She knew she should do something to put out the flames licking up inside of her, but all such resolve seemed to go up in smoke. Leaning into his embrace, she gave in to the urge to run her fingers down the hard plane of his jaw. Then, as if knowing that in another instant she would be consumed by the fire, she managed to draw back. Her hands came up against his chest. "I . . . think you had better take me home, sir."

"Gus," he began.

"Please! At once!" She was mortified by the note of rising panic in her voice. Flighty heroines and gothic melodramas had always seemed so laughable to her, yet here she was, enacting her own Cheltenham tragedy. It would have been a most amusing scene, she supposed, had she not been the leading lady.

Sheffield looked at her uncertainly. "I'm sorry but—"

The sound of an approaching carriage only threatened to turn high drama into farce.

The little tiger, who had studiously kept his eyes averted from what was going on in the front of the vehicle cleared his throat. "Er, guv. There's somebody coming up on us fast. Ye might want te replace wot's in yer hands with the reins, if ye knows wot's good fer ye."

The earl's response was a rather long curse.

"Don't go yelling at me," muttered the tiger "I ain't the one drivin' the udder team." He gave an affronted sniff. "Nor is I the one what's been doing the kissing." His breath came out in a doleful sigh. "Wimmen!"

Sheffield bit back another oath as he made to follow his tiger's advice. He snatched up the reins and set his own horses in motion just as the other carriage came tooling around the bend. There was no room to pass and so it was forced to slow down until the the trees were cleared and the path widened once again. Lord Wilford gave a brief wave as he swung out to pass. The other occupants—two maiden aunts and a spotty-faced younger sibling just down from Oxford—nodded as they went by.

Augusta studiously avoided their speculative gazes while silently giving thanks that the current state of her bonnet and dress were as easily due to the brisk breeze encountered in an open carriage as to any other cause. The park was rapidly filling with other vehicles, making all but the most banal conversation impossible. As neither of them seemed inclined to revert to such topics, the drive home was accompanied by naught but the sound of the jingling harnesses and the cadence of the matched team.

On drawing to halt in front of her townhouse, the earl hesitated in dismounting. "I'm sorry if I upset you." His eyes seemed to be searching her face for something. "Perhaps we had best . . . talk about what is happening."

That was the last thing in the world she wished to do. "Perhaps we had best try to avoid letting it happen again," she snapped. "Obviously, the heat of the chase is affecting our reason."

If she didn't know better, she would have thought she detected a look of hurt in his eyes. But whatever had been there was quickly masked by a cool detachment that matched her own. "Ah, you think that is what it is?"

"What else could it be?" There was a fraction of a pause. "At least for me. You, no doubt, are quite using to stealing kisses in carriages." She stared down at her tightly clasped fingers. "I imagine if it had been—" She caught herself, aghast at the words that had been about to slip out. Of course he would rather have kissed Marianne. She didn't blame him in the least, for any man would. But she would never wish to reveal to anyone, much less the earl, how much that hurt.

"If it had been what?" he asked quietly.

"If . . . if it had been any female, the result would have been the same," she stammered.

"Goddamn son of a poxed whore!" Though the words were barely audible, she could see that he was truly angry. "Bloody hell," he added for good measure. "You have read all my letters and yet you insist on seeing me as nothing more than a profligate wastrel? Then perhaps your depth of understanding runs only as deep as ink on paper, for in person you show remarkably little perception or empathy." His jaw worked slightly. "Your intellect may be unassailable, but in matters of feeling, you should think twice about signing yourself as Firebrand. In truth, you are as hard and cold as ice." He threw down the reins and climbed down without further words.

It was all Augusta could do to keep from bursting

into tears as he escorted her up the marble stairs. He was wrong. Her intellect was as suspect as her emotions. She was a fool—a bloody fool, to borrow his words. Now she had lost everything that mattered, her best friend as well as her heart.

And she thought she was so clever. With such hubris, she supposed she deserved what she got.

As Sheffield gave a rap with the brass knocker, she asked in a small voice, "About Lord Ludlowe . . ."

"If you mean, will I abandon the quest for justice, you may be assured I will not succumb to boredom and walk away from the matter."

She didn't dare look at him. "But what do you intend to do?" she went on, her eyes locked on the hem of her dress.

There was a moment of silence. "Perhaps I'll send you a note to keep you informed," he replied coldly.

The door swung open.

"Good day, Miss Hadley." He turned and his boots beat a staccato retreat on the polished stone.

Augusta went inside, barely aware of the butler's greeting or of how she managed to put one foot in front of the other. As she passed by the drawing room, her mother appeared in the doorway, a broad smile on her lips.

"Augusta, my dear!"

She dragged to a reluctant halt, her ears hardly registering the rare endearment. "Yes, Mama?"

"You sly puss. Here I thought Marianne was the one who was going to make the splendid match."

Augusta stared in some confusion. "Marianne is engaged? She said nothing to me about—"

"Oh, do stop teasing, my dear. You know my constitution has not allowed me to go out very often these past few weeks, but I have just heard the most interesting news from Lady Framingham about the attentions a certain gentleman has been paying to you. And now I see for myself that the gossips have not been exaggerating. I vow, I hadn't dreamed it possible you could be so clever! When do we expect an announcement?"

Augusta looked utterly perplexed. "An announcement of what?"

"Why, of your betrothal to Lord Sheffield."

A look of disbelief crossed her face. "You must be joking," she blurted out, even though she knew her mother had precious little sense of humor, especially not on the subject of marriage. "I assure you, Mama, Lord Sheffield has no intention of legshackling himself to me."

"Don't use such horrid cant," snapped her mother out of habit. Then her brow puckered in distress. "What do you mean? The carriage rides, the marked preference at balls—"

"They have nothing to do with the earl's interest in me personally, Mama. We have merely been trying to solve an . . . intellectual problem."

Disappointment made her mother's words even harsher. "Unnatural child," she huffed. " A chance to attach a man such as Sheffield and you can think of nothing but your silly books and stupid theories? How many times do I have to tell you that men don't find a bluestocking at all attractive?"

"I'm well aware of that fact," she answered in a near whisper.

Her mother heaved a grumpy sigh. "Well, maybe it isn't too late. Maybe the earl has suffered some heavy losses at the gaming table and is desperate for a large dowry. At least you have *that*."

Augusta's eyes pressed closed. "I doubt it would be near large enough."

"What was that?"

"Nothing, Mama."

"Hmmph." Her mother started back toward the settee and her tea tray. "Do try to act like a normal female when you are with him. And try not to give him a disgust of you with your odd whims and notions."

She hung her head. "Yes, Mama," was about the

only answer she could manage. Why bother informing her parent that it was much too late for that. Why, the moon would turn into a wheel of Stilton before the Earl of Sheffield would cast another look at her. With such a lowering thought in mind, she hurried on into the sanctuary of her study and flung her bonnet and reticule aside. Only then, seated at her desk, head buried in her arms, did she allow the bitter tears to flow.

Through the muffled sobs, she did not hear the sound of the door opening and closing a short time later. It was not until a gentle touch steadied her quivering shoulder that she was aware of Marianne's presence in the room.

"Oh Gus, whatever is wrong?" asked her sister.

Augusta didn't look up. "Please, Marianne. Right now I just want to be alone."

Her sister refused to be put off so easily. "Do you? I doubt it. You've always been a source of comfort and wisdom to me when I am upset. Why won't you let me try to be the same?"

"Wisdom! Hah! What a charlatan I am to give advice." There was a waver in her voice. "Why, I'm the biggest fool of all, always thinking I have the answer."

Marianne was tactfully silent as Augusta searched for a handkerchief in her pocket and blew her nose. Then she ventured a tentative smile. "You always say it helps to talk things out in a rational manner. And you are usually right. Things never seem quite as dreadful after one does."

Augusta brushed at her cheek with her sleeve. "Do I really say that? Then I'm more of an idiot than I imagined. What really makes one feel better is falling into a fit of vapors." Her mouth finally managed to form a rueful grimace. "I have considerably more sympathy for all those brainless heroines who turn into watering pots at the slightest provocation. Perhaps they are onto something."

Marianne stifled a giggle.

She blew her nose again. "In fact, I think I shall curl up for the rest of the afternoon with one of Mrs. Radcliffe's horrid novels and thoroughly enjoy all the rantings and weepings."

"Well, I am glad to see your normal sense of humor reasserting itself."

"Actually I'm being quite serious."

There was a moment of silence, then both of them couldn't repress a soft burst of laughter.

"Dear Gus," murmured Marianne, giving her a quick hug as their laughter subsided. "Now out with it. What happened between you and Lord Sheffield that has you in such a rare taking?" Seeing that Augusta's spirits seemed sufficiently recovered, she essayed a bit of quizzing. "A lover's quarrel?"

That was perhaps not the best tack to take. Augusta's expression immediately lost any glimmer of her usual self. "Hardly. For that would imply there was any romantic interest in the first place." She couldn't repress a ragged sigh. "We did, however, have a certain . . . friendship, but now I'm afraid I've managed to destroy that. He finds me totally repugnant and wants nothing more to do with me."

"Gus, I'm sure that is not true. I am under the distinct impression that Lord Sheffield is, er, not adverse to your company."

"It *is* true. Last night he called me a stubborn, willful t-t-termagant." Her voice had begun to quiver. "And that is not the worst of it. Today he said—" The words were lost in a snuffle.

Her sister made a number of sympathetic sounds as she patted Augusta's hand. "Well, that wasn't very gentlemanly of him, but I'm sure he will make a handsome apology—"

"No, he won't. I've said enough dreadful things to him that he will never forgive me." She was forced to stop, in order to blink back another wave of tears that was threatening to spill. "Why am I so awkward and outspoken? I . . . I wish I could be more like you—

you find it so easy to be charming, to make people smile and feel at ease." She turned a watery glance at Marianne's lovely profile. "No doubt Alex would have much preferred driving out with you instead of me. He . . . mentioned that he found your company quite pleasant last night—unlike mine."

Her sister wisely avoided any comment on the use of the earl's Christian name. But her expression darkened on listening to the last little confession. "Gus, now you *are* beginning to sound like one of the widget-headed heroines in those ridiculous books. Never say you wish to be like anyone else. I may be fortunate to be endowed with looks that gentlemen seem to find attractive, but that is hardly a credit to any of my own accomplishments. You, on the other hand, have had the wits and the courage to form your own character. You are not awkward and outspoken, rather a unique individual with a style all your own and the strength to stand up for your convictions."

Augusta was rendered momentarily speechless by her sister's passionate words.

"And furthermore, as to the earl's enjoying my company, I'll have you know what he wanted to talk with me about was *you*."

"Me! Whatever for?"

Marianne thought for an moment, torn between not wanting to lie and not wanting to ruin the plan to keep her sister out of danger. "Ah . . . he was inquiring as to whether I thought you might be convinced to act a little . . . less rashly in regard to your investigation."

No doubt the earl had been referring to more than that, thought Augusta as she pulled a face. "Well, unfortunately I seem unable to curb my rash behavior, no matter what the situation." She bit her lip and her fingers began to fiddle with the pen on her desk. "I shall try very hard in the future to stop and think before I act—or speak."

Her sister didn't miss the note of wistful regret in her voice. "Are you sure you don't wish to tell me exactly what caused the unpleasantness between you and Lord Sheffield this afternoon?"

She drew the nib of the pen across a sheet of blank paper, leaving nothing but a thin scar across the surface. "It's rather . . . complicated."

"Then I won't press you, if you truly do not wish to speak of it." Marianne brushed an errant curl from her cheek. "But as I said, I imagine you are exaggerating any disagreements with His Lordship. I'd be willing to wager that when you see him tonight at the Yarmouths' ball, the two of you will manage to straighten things out."

Augusta shook her head. "I mean to cry off from going. I simply don't feel up to facing an evening of festivities at the moment."

Marianne fixed her with a look that mingled concern with a certain suspicion. "Gus, I trust you are not contemplating anything, well, rash?"

"Don't worry. Do go along and dress, for I know you have been looking forward to the evening. I promise I am not contemplating anything stupid."

That, of course, was a matter of opinion.

Sheffield was already regretting his harsh words as he took up his perch and guided his team back toward his townhouse. She had not deserved such a stinging setdown. It was not her fault that a simmering desire had left his feelings rather raw and vulnerable, just as it was not her fault that she obviously felt no such heated emotions toward him.

Arrogant coxcomb, he berated himself, to imagine that simply because he wished it, she would fall willingly into his arms, like the legion of ladies before her.

Worse than that, he was a fool, for he had let his damnable temper cause him to lose his best friend. He had not failed to see all expression drain from her face at his cruel words and the way her eyes could not even hazard a glance in his direction after such ungentlemanly behavior. While she might have held

some admiration and regard for the person she knew
on paper, no doubt she now felt only scorn and disgust
for the flesh and blood fellow he turned out to be.

Could he blame her?

From the very beginning it was, as she had said,
like flint striking steel every time they met. Sparks
flew, and though they ignited a certain heat as well, at
least in his loins, they usually lit up his worst qualities.
Odious. Arrogant. Overbearing. He had been all those
things and more whenever they met—and argued. No
wonder she hardly welcomed his embraces. Would he
ever be able to win the same trust and honesty in
real life that his pen had garnered with the scratch of
a nib?

He drew in a long breath. And what did it matter?
He had told himself he was helping the feisty Miss
Hadley out of regard for her late brother, but it was
becoming increasingly clear that the reason was not
nearly so simple as that. Up until very recently, he
had studiously avoided probing into his true feelings,
perhaps because he feared what he would find.

Tired of a superficial life, devoid of all challenge or
meaning, he had sought to commit himself wholly to
something that mattered. The correspondence with
Firebrand had only sparked his determination to find
a new direction for his considerable energy. What he
hadn't anticipated was that more than his intellect
would be kindled into a white-hot intensity. And he
wasn't sure he was ready to make that sort of
commitment.

Miss Hadley. Sharp-tongued, opinioned, and possibly more stubborn than he was. She was hardly the
type of female that should send a heat coursing
through his veins. Yet he also knew she was much
more than that. Intelligent, perceptive, and capable of
great compassion and courage, as she had shown on
paper as well as in her determined quest for justice.
He found himself unable to describe the feeling she

elicited from him, no doubt because he had never met anyone like her before.

Stifling an oath, he drew to a halt in front of his steps and turned the team over to his tiger. It appeared that not only did he need to solve Miss Hadley's mystery but the conundrum of his own heart in the bargain.

"Er, she is not here, sir." At the look of exasperation that crossed the earl's features, Marianne hastened to add, "She was feeling a bit fatigued and decided to spend a quiet night at home."

His brows drew together.

"She did promise she would not do anything stupid. In fact, those were her exact words."

"I don't like the sound of that," he growled. "Not one bit. It is just the sort of thing she would say when she—" His words cut off sharply as a liveried footman approached.

"Lord Sheffield?"

At his curt nod, the man discreetly pressed a note into the earl's glove while handing him a glass of champagne. "There was an urchin below who insisted this be delivered to you immediately, my lord."

Chapter Fourteen

Guv, I think you had best come quick. The lady
in question has just left her house.

Choking back a string of curses that would likely
have seared the younger Miss Hadley's ears, the
earl quickly tucked the scrap of paper in his waistcoat
pocket while taking a swallow of the champagne. Then
carefully schooling his features to mask his inner agita-
tion, he set the glass aside.

"Oh dear," whispered Marianne, not failing to note
the slight tightening of his jaw. "Has Gus . . ." She
left the question dangling.

Sheffield made a deliberate adjustment of his
starched cuff. "Do not alarm yourself, Miss Hadley,"
he answered in a low voice. But he added no further
explanation as his gaze scanned over the crowded
room. His eyes narrowed slightly on failing to spot
what he was looking for, but in the fashionable crush,
he couldn't be certain. He had at least managed to
catch the attention of his young cousin, who had been
hovering nearby.

The young man hurriedly quit a circle of young
bucks ogling a particularly well-endowed miss on the
dance floor and came to stand by the earl's shoulder.

"Lucas, I trust you will see that Miss Hadley has a
pleasant evening and that she and her mother are escorted to their carriage." The note of command was
unmistakable in his tone.

"Of course, sir."

"But—" began Marianne.

"I fear I am called away by a trifling matter." He fixed her with a pointed look. "But I have no doubt that I shall be able to see to it without causing any need for worry."

Marianne ceased any further protest. "Yes," she said slowly. "I trust that you are capable of handling any problem you may face."

Andover looked slightly confused at the odd exchange, but kept a prudent silence as Sheffield yielded his place by Marianne's side.

"There is no cause for concern, Miss Hadley," the earl added on noting that despite her words, her face had gone a shade paler. "I shall see to everything."

No cause for concern, he repeated to himself as he left the ballroom. Hah! The maddening minx. What was she up to this time? He forced his steps to remain unrushed, though a mixture of anger, exasperation, and fear had kindled a blaze of impatience in his breast. Once out on the street, he picked up his pace considerably, threading in and out of the clog of carriages in a rush to locate his own. The man he had employed to keep an eye on Augusta would be waiting for him at the corner of the park and, from the tone of his hastily scrawled note, there didn't appear to be any time to waste. So intent was he on deciding his next move that he didn't notice the two cloaked men who had slipped up behind him until the cold barrel of a pistol was jammed into his ribs.

"Get in the carriage, m'lord."

A nondescript vehicle, undistinguished by any markings, had slowed to a stop and the door was jerked open. Sheffield hesitated a fraction, but a rough hand tightened its hold on his coat and shoved him forward. "Quickly, else it'll go worse fer ye, I promise."

There seemed little choice but to comply. He turned to climb in, and as he did, the butt of the weapon came down on his head with a sickening thud.

*   *   *

Augusta peered up at the darkened window and swallowed the rising lump in her throat. At home, in the warm confines of her study, it had seemed like a reasonable decision. But now, alone in the deserted alleyway, she found herself fighting the urge to turn tail and abandon her plan.

Coward, she chastised herself. Just because she hadn't ever undertaken this sort of thing without the reassuring presence of Jamison was no reason to panic. She was perfectly capable of climbing to a window ledge and freeing the catch of the window by herself. And hadn't she proven she could pick a desk lock as well as any thief? The memory of that night came flooding back and she allowed herself a tiny smile at the recollection of how she and the earl had been forced to work together in order to cover the real reason for the break-in. Her amusement turned into something warmer as she also recalled the heat of his muscled form pressed hard on top of hers.

With a firm shake of her head, she sought to banish all such thoughts. It was abundantly clear she would never again enjoy a camaraderie with the earl in any endeavor, not even on paper. Her mother was right. She was a most unnatural female—tall, ungainly, outspoken, with not a single attribute that a gentleman would find attractive, unless one counted money as a particular charm.

Well, the Earl of Sheffield did not need money. And he certainly had no other reason to want her. His words burned once again in her ears, each one singeing a little piece of her heart.

Cold. Shallow. Opinionated.

Augusta blinked back a tear. He might find her all those things, but she was at least determined to prove to him there was nothing wrong with her capacity for clever planning, no matter her other faults. Perhaps if she managed to get hold of the concrete evidence to prove Lord Ludlowe's perfidy, he would end up considering her not totally unworthy of regard.

Not that it would change things between them.

Her own sharp tongue had cut through whatever tenuous bond had been forged between them and no amount of remorse could repair the damage. Never again would she feel the warmth of his hand at the small of her back, just as never again would she read the elegant script that those strong capable fingers could pen.

A stray cat brushed up against her leg, nearly drawing an audible cry from her lips. With shaking hands, Augusta pulled the heavy cloak tighter around her shoulders and sought to quiet the pounding of her heart. After several minutes, she was able to steady both her nerves and her resolve to go ahead with her plan.

Her own heartache was nothing in comparison to the pain and uncertainty that her friends were feeling. That was what mattered right now. She must put aside all mooning over the earl and concentrate on seeing that the monstrous scheme concocted by Lord Ludlowe was put to an end.

She made a methodical check for the picklocks, candle, and pistol in her pockets, then patted at the bulge of the second small pistol tucked in the waistband of her breeches at the small of her back. All was in readiness. Drawing another deep breath, she stole from the shadows and slipped into the gated garden.

"May the devil rut with a two-faced sheep."

His voice still groggy, Sheffield struggled to a sitting position and rubbed at the nasty lump on the back of his head. It took him a moment to realize he was no longer in the back of a carriage but lying on a thick Oriental carpet.

"Really, Sheffield. Hardly the sort of language for a fine gentleman to use in refined company."

The earl sought to bring his hazy surroundings into focus. Shaking his woozy head, he was slowly able to make out the barrel of the pistol pointed at his chest,

then the glass of brandy that was held nonchalantly
in the other hand, then finally the face that sneered
down at him from the cushioned comfort of the
leather wing chair. Ludlowe crossed his legs and took
a leisurely sip of the amber spirits.

Another oath, this one even more graphic than the
first, slipped from Sheffield's lips.

The other man laughed. "Your eloquent tongue will
do you little good now. I warned you not to meddle
in any of this, but you wouldn't cease your rantings
in Parliament. Now it's far too late. You've become
too great of a threat to me."

Sheffield winced as he sought to remain upright.
Hell's teeth, he cursed at himself. He should have
been more alert, but he had been so worried about
Augusta that he had failed to pay attention to any
lurking danger. It had been stupid on his part, but at
least the current situation would seem to assure that
she would be safe from harm. Not even the headstrong
Miss Hadley would be so foolhardy as to attempt to
break into a house that was obviously occupied.

His attention turned back to his own predicament.
Measuring the distance between himself and Ludlowe,
he saw there was little chance of making a lunge for
the man, especially in his present condition. But perhaps if he could keep the fellow talking for a bit, an
opportunity would present itself. In the meantime, he
needed some time to clear his head. "A threat? So
why didn't your men simply stick a knife in my ribs
and be done with it?" he asked. "Or did they bungle
the attempt yet again?"

Ludlowe's lips compressed in some irritation. "That
harridan Miss Hadley is not around this time to save
your neck." He took another swallow of his drink and
seemed to relax slightly. "Can't imagine what you
have been doing in her presence," he continued in a
slow drawl. "From what I witnessed, she quite proved
her reputation for having a sharp tongue, not to speak

of that ungainly height and angular face. A real Amazon." He grimaced. "You've a reputation for good taste in ladies, and Lord knows, you don't need the blunt. I, on the other hand, have need of a plump dowry, so I shall have to force myself to pretend a continued interest until I have wed the chit. Bedding her will be an onerous chore—" A rustle of the draperies caused him to pause, but only for a moment. "Yet with such a willful spirit, maybe it will prove an interesting diversion, at least until I've broken her to saddle." He exaggerated a shudder. "But with any luck, I'll beget an heir on her quickly and can turn my attention to females more to my taste."

It was only with the greatest of difficulty that Sheffield restrained the urge to lunge at the man's neck, regardless of the distance, and throttle the life from him. "There was no female to stop the bullet earlier tonight," he said through gritted teeth, controlling his anger by telling himself he might learn something of use. "Why risk bringing me here?"

Ludlowe regarded him coolly from over his drink. "Yes, I admit the first few tries were meant to send you to your Maker forthwith. But the plan had to be, shall we say altered."

"Really? For what reason?"

The glass swirled slowly, spinning the contents into a vortex of amber and gold. It was as if the motion itself tugged Ludlowe's mouth down into a smug sneer. "Changed tailors recently?"

The earl pressed his eyes closed for an instant and cursed himself for an even bigger fool that before. In his haste to inform Augusta of his discovery, he had not considered that the obscure tailor would reveal his inquiries so quickly. And he had accused *her* of acting without thinking of the consequences!

Ludlowe brushed a speck of dust from his embroidered waistcoat and went on. "The nodcock couldn't wait to let me know how such an arbiter of style as yourself had admired my choice of silk. Careless of you, Sheffield. But then again, you have never showed much aptitude for cleverness. Too busy using other parts of your anatomy." He paused once again, this time to refill his glass. "The ladies, no doubt, shall miss you. However, before I speed you to your eternal rest, I need several answers."

Sheffield's lips curled slightly. "Is that so?"

Ludlowe seemed to miss the note of irony. "Yes. At first I thought your speeches were a mere whim, but now it appears you know all too much about my activities for it to be coincidence. Who else is involved with you? Who was it that discovered the piece of my waistcoat?" He frowned. "It was unfortunate that a last-minute change of plans made it necessary for me to be involved in the actual dirty work that day. The man who usually took care of that part of the business had broken his arm in a tavern brawl the night before, but he had staked out the place and rather than miss the opportunity to grab such a strong lad, I decided to take the chance of doing it myself. The damn brat struggled like a hellion, and I didn't dare linger once I'd knocked him unconscious, as several of the nearby farmhands were about to quit for the day."

"Careless of you, Ludlowe."

This time the mockery was unmistakable. The other man's mouth hardened. He stood up and sauntered over to where the earl was lying. "You are in no position to make glib taunts," he snarled, delivering a vicious kick to Sheffield's ribs. "You are also going to tell me the identity of that other rabblerouser who is stirring up the public's interest. Firebrand—" He fairly spat the word out. "The bastard is even more trouble than you are. But I shall deal with him soon enough."

The earl gave a curt laugh, ignoring the stab of pain that shot through his abdomen. "Firebrand? Why, no one knows who he is."

"The two of you share too many ideas not to have

had some contact with each other. My guess is you know very well who the cur is."

Sheffield shrugged. "What makes you think I would tell you even if I did?"

Ludlowe reached out and pressed the muzzle of the gun hard up against Sheffield's temple and cocked the trigger.

"Hardly a threat with teeth, seeing as I am to shuffle off this mortal coil regardless of whether I speak or not."

The barrel caught him a blow to the mouth, drawing a trickle of blood. "Oh, there are ways to make you talk, Sheffield, and believe me, I shall enjoy every minute of it. Have you ever seen the thin scalpels the Chinese use to flay the flesh from troublesome peasants? In another hour, you will be begging me to put a bullet in your brain." Ludlowe brandished the weapon in the air. "Now, I'll give you one last chance to tell me what I want to know. If you do, I'll promise to make your death a painless one."

Sheffield appeared to give the offer deep thought for several moments. A resigned sigh followed. "Oh, very well. I suppose it is pointless to fight the inevitable. You seem to have been smarter than all of us." Though the chances of escaping seemed to be slipping away, he sought to keep the man talking. Something might occur that would allow him to make use of what he learned. "There is one thing I should like to know. How do you manage to run such a deucedly clever operation without anyone discovering what you are up to? Where do the children end up?"

Ludlowe circled back to his chair and tossed back the last of his brandy. Unable to resist the chance to gloat in his triumph, he came back to tower over the earl's prostrate form. "Actually it was quite simple . . ." He went on to explain in great detail how he chose where to strike, how he organized his henchmen, and how he effected the transport of the kidnapped children north. "You were getting quite close to the truth," he finished. "The brats go into several mines where none but the smallest bodies can work. It makes, shall we say, for a profitable arrangement for everyone."

"Save for the children," muttered Sheffield under his breath. In a louder voice he added, "Very clever indeed. Let me guess—the mines belong to Herter and Gollert?"

Ludlowe grinned. "Thurgood and Manning."

"Ah."

"And now the name of your informant in the country. And that miscreant Firebrand."

The earl shrugged. "As I told you, he could be anyone."

The polished boot connected once again with Sheffield's middle, this time drawing an audible grunt. As it drew back to deliver another blow, the distinct click of a pistol being cocked sounded from somewhere near the heavy damask draperies.

"I think that is quite enough, Ludlowe."

Caught off guard, with his own weapon dangling carelessly in one hand, the man staggered back a few steps.

"Goddamn son of a poxed whore!"

"Really, sir! I should think under the circumstances your greeting might be a tad friendlier than that," said Augusta, her eyes never wavering from Ludlowe's shocked face as she stepped into the circle of light cast by the branch of candles. "Drop your weapon," she barked at the man.

He hesitated.

"I am accorded to be a good shot, and in fact I should welcome the slightest excuse to pull the trigger, you miserable cur."

Ludlowe's eyes narrowed, but the weapon dropped to the floor.

Augusta shot a quick glance at the earl. "Are you all right?"

"I suppose I shall live. What were you waiting for— the knives to come out?" he grumbled.

"I was tempted. Perhaps a little judicious bleeding would prove the cure to your nasty temper," she shot back. "Anyway, you would not have had me interrupt before you had coaxed all the evidence out, would you?" She took a step closer to him. "That was very clever of you, by the way."

"Delighted you approve."

"What the devil is going on here," cried Ludlowe in some confusion.

Augusta smiled sweetly. "The harridan has come around once again to save Sheffield's neck"

"I would have thought of something myself," he groused. "And as for your showing up here! Didn't I make it clear you were not to attempt any more of your impulsive, corkbrained, dangerous stunts—"

"Well, you should be glad I did, seeing as you allowed them to pluck you from the streets as easily as they did." She paused for a fraction. "Careless of you, Sheffield."

"I was in a damned hurry because I was rushing to come after *you*." He rubbed at the lump on his head and gave another wince.

"How did you know what I was doing?"

There was a slight cough. "Er, we'll discuss that some other time."

Ludlowe had been staring at them in growing disbelief during the short exchange. "My God! This shrew lives at Greenfield Manor. She must be the one who told you, but I can't believe a female would have had the brains to figure it out."

The earl gave a grim smile. "It is all very well to disparage my intelligence, but you made a grave mistake in underestimating Miss Hadley."

"Not likely." The other man had inched toward his desk.

"Augusta, watch out for—" began the earl.

With a flick of his wrist Ludlowe sent the branch of

candles flying onto Sheffield's lap. As Augusta gasped and took an involuntary step forward, her attention riveted on the sparks and flames threatening to set the earl's breeches on fire, Ludlowe lunged at her and was able to wrest the pistol from her grasp. "Intelligence?" he snarled, pushing her away from him. "No more than you. Indeed, the two of you gudgeons make quite a matched pair."

Sheffield slowly levered himself up from the floor, having easily put out the flames. "Think on it, Ludlowe," he warned. "My demise you might arrange to look the work of footpads, but two deaths will raise any number of awkward questions. Let Miss Hadley go. She has no proof against you, and who is going to take the word of a sharp-tongued, old female—" Augusta's eyes blazed with indignation—"over that of a gentleman."

Ludlowe gave a nasty laugh. "On the contrary, Sheffield. There will be nary a troublesome question. The two of you have just given me a perfect opportunity to rid myself of your meddlings with no risk to me at all." He paused, savoring his cleverness. "You see, in the course of doing business, I have made certain acquaintances at out-of-the-way inns who, for a price, will be happy to turn a blind eye on anything that might occur in the dead of night—even several shots." He gave a mock sigh. "No doubt it will give the tabbies food for gossip for months when it is learned that the unfortunate Miss Hadley allowed herself to be seduced by the Earl of Sheffield, only to put a bullet in him when she learned he had no intention of continuing on to Gretna Green. No one will be surprised that she then was driven by remorse and shame to take her own life. I have already begun to compose the note."

Augusta gave an audible gasp and staggered forward several steps. Her hand came up to clutch at her throat. "I . . . I am feeling very faint."

"Catch her before she keels over," ordered Ludlowe. His lip curled in contempt. "Hysterical harpy. You'll soon feel worse than faint, but for the moment, I need you in one piece."

The earl reached out and Augusta fell back into his arms, so hard that her dead weight caused a woof of air to come from his lips. For good measure, she flailed her arms and squirmed in a fit of vapors, taking care to rub her back hard up against Sheffield's middle.

His arms came firmly around her waist, but one hand slowly stole under her cloak. "Close your eyes and go limp," he whispered in her ear as his fingers found the weapon hidden in her waistband. In a louder voice, he addressed the other man. "She's passed out cold. Allow me to lay her on the floor—she's damn heavy."

Ludlowe motioned for him to go ahead.

Sheffield put her down, then slowly rose. While still in a crouch, he whipped up the gun and squeezed off a quick shot. The bullet caught Ludlowe in the arm, sending his own weapon clattering to the floor. Augusta slithered across the carpet in a trice and grabbed it up.

"Meddlesome old bluestocking!" cried Ludlowe, clutching at his bloodied sleeve. "I shall—"

Sheffield's fist slammed into the other man's jaw.

There was a mere wisp of a groan as Ludlowe crumpled to the floor.

Augusta scrambled to her feet, the weapon still cocked and ready. "I was sorely tempted to pull the trigger."

"I know, but it is best this way. We will let the authorities deal with him. He won't escape the noose." He held out his hand. "Give me the pistol, Gus. I shall see to him."

She gave a resigned sigh and handed it over. "I suppose you are right." Her eyes traveled slowly to the unconscious form lying in a heap on the carpet, then to the earl's glowering face. "I wish I knew how to do that."

Sheffield's features relaxed into a lopsided grin. "Your knowledge is quite extensive enough without knowing how to go a few rounds with Jackson. Besides, I fear I should probably end up the main target, and your prowess with lemonade is lethal enough."

A moment of awkward silence followed. He fiddled with the gun, then lay it aside. "Gus—" he began.

"I know. You wish to ring a peal over my head," she said in a rush, "but—"

His hand came up to graze her cheek, causing her words to catch in her throat. "A peal? Yes, I suppose I do," he said softly, though there was some emotion other than anger in his voice. "Don't *ever* scare me like that again. The thought of you racing neck and leather into such danger had me half mad."

Augusta's mouth twisted into a rueful grimace. "Not half mad, I'm sure. Entirely mad."

"You should never have entered this room."

"Well, it was too late. I was already here when the two of you, er, made an appearance."

"You could have slipped back out the window."

She couldn't keep her eyes from jerking up to meet his. "And leave you here at Ludlowe's mercy?"

For an instant, an expression flashed in the hazel depths that made Sheffield dare to hope all was not lost between them.

Her thumb came up to touch lightly at the corner of his mouth. "You are hurt. I'm sorry I had to let him go on like that with you, but it was vital that he tell us everything."

"Leaving me in his clutches would have been what I deserved, considering—" he began, only to be interrupted by the muffled sound of pounding at the front door. At the same time, a head appeared at the mullioned window and there was a tapping at the glass. Swearing under his breath, the earl went over and flung it open.

"When ye didn't show up, guv, I took the liberty of sending fer Bow Street. Stevie stuck te the lady, like ye's ordered, and follered her here." A scruffy looking fellow craned his neck and took in the fallen form of Ludlowe. "Look's like ye got things settled without der help, but at the sound of the shots they's gone ahead and broken in the front door."

"You did the right thing, Jones." The earl turned to Augusta. "You had best be out of here before they come in," he said softly. "My man will see you safely home."

"But we must search the desk for further proof, and question—"

The tramp of hurried steps echoed from the hallway. "You may trust me to do all those things. Please don't argue with me on this, Gus." Sheffield took her arm and drew her toward the window. His mouth quirked into a faint smile. "Now, if you will just leave the way you came in."

She swung one foot up over the sill. "Will you promise to . . . send around a note and let me know what happens?"

He nodded. "I promise you will hear of everything."

The other leg went up, and Jones reached to help her down.

"Gus."

She turned around.

His lips came down hard on hers for an instant, then he propelled her into the other man's waiting arms.

Augusta paced back and forth before the fire, her eyes straying to the clock on the mantel every few minutes. "Damnation," she muttered aloud. It was nearly midmorning and she still had no word from the earl. Surely he could have taken the time to pen a short note to inform her that the culprit was finally locked away and the authorities were beginning to move against the unscrupulous mines.

She sighed. No doubt it would be the last bit of

correspondence she would ever receive from him.
Wandering back to her desk, she picked a letter at
random from the neat pile lying on the blotter and
began to read. Each word on the paper seemed to
burn a hole in her heart. Lord, she would miss their
intimate exchange of thoughts.

But even more, she would miss his company in the
flesh. It felt as if he had become almost a part of her,
yet she must resign herself to giving him up, no matter
how much the void ached. They were too different to
fit together comfortably. Hadn't she seen the sparks
fly often enough to know that? And hadn't their hot
words left raw scars on each other? She mustn't fool
herself into thinking his kiss of last night was fired by
anything other than the heat of the chase.

A discreet knock on the door caused her to brush
a tear from her cheek. She hastily shoved all of the
letters into the top drawer and pushed it closed. At
least, she would have the pleasure of seeing his distinctive script once more. "Come in, Jenkins," she called.
"I have been waiting for—"

Her words died in her throat as Sheffield entered
instead of the butler.

"Oh!" Augusta turned to hide the quiver of her lips.

"I thought you would like to know what the authorities are planning." He shifted his weight from one
foot to the other. "It would have entailed a rather
long letter, so I thought I might as well stop by
myself."

"Of course."

"With what Ludlowe told us last night and the number of documents found in his desk, there will be no
trouble in arresting the owners of the mines. His co-
horts will find their way to the gallows as well. And
the children will be returned to their families." He
gave a sigh. "Though I fear not all."

"No." This time, at least, she had a good excuse for
the tear that spilled to one cheek. "We could not save
them all. I . . . I wish I could have done more." She

reached up to brush it away, but the earl was suddenly close by and his fingers came up gently against her skin.

"You have done more than any one person could be expected to do. Not only did you stop this monster, but your eloquent writings have raised the public's awareness of the horrors of child labor enough so that it may never happen again."

"But . . . but much of the credit for that rests with you as well."

"Only because you encouraged me to take action."

Augusta drew in a long breath and looked away into the fire. "It doesn't really matter who is responsible. All that counts is that Ludlowe has been stopped."

"He is safely locked away in Newgate." Sheffield was so close to her shoulder that she could feel the warmth of him through her gown. She started to move away but his hand touched her arm. "Gus. About last night . . ."

"You needn't apologize. I know the heat of the chase makes us do things we wouldn't normally do."

He stared at her for several moments. "You know, the heat of the chase is now over."

"Yes, I suppose it is."

His arms came around her. "Then why do you suppose this is happening?" he murmured as his lips grazed over her cheekbone.

"I . . . I don't know."

"Mmmmm. Take an educated guess." A gossamer kiss lingered on the lobe of her ear.

Her legs suddenly felt very wobbly. "But you do not even like me! You said—"

"You are all too aware of my damnable temper. I say a good deal of things I don't mean when I am angry. And even worse things when I am hurt."

Augusta bit her lip. "I hurt you?"

"You seemed so indifferent to me in the flesh. It was hard to bear, as I desperately wanted you to care for the real me as much as you seemed to esteem my ghost on paper."

"Oh, Alex." Her arms had stolen up around his neck and she pressed her face against his shoulder. "If I acted indifferently it was because I was afraid to show you even a hint of how much I had come to . . . esteem you. I thought you might find an aging, ungainly spinster's attention unwelcome."

"You think yourself unattractive, Gus?" He gave a soft laugh. "At last I have found a subject about which you are totally wrong."

"But I am too . . . sharp in all the wrong places."

"No, my dear, you are exactly right in every way. Sharp where it counts, soft and rounded just where you should be." He tilted her chin up and ran his mouth along the line of her jaw.

"I . . . I suppose I must defer to your greater knowledge in these things."

He gave a chuckle. "A wise decision."

Augusta was silent for moment. "Does this mean we can still be friends? That is, can we still correspond like before?"

"I am afraid not."

She tried to hide the disappointment that pinched at her face.

"You see, my man of affairs has said I am spending far too much on ink and paper." He gave a crooked grin. "So I really must insist that we continue our relationship in the flesh rather than in letters, my dear. If you remember, I had suggested that we meet to discuss our ideas over a glass of port—would you care to make that every night?" His grin widened, though there was a touch of vulnerability beneath the humor. "Although I'm afraid it would have to be our own library, for White's is out of the question."

The light that came to Augusta's eyes put his fears to rest. "For now, perhaps," she answered, a mischievous smile of her own stealing across her features. "However, our next crusade could be—"

He interrupted with a mock groan. "And my friends already think I am a candidate for Bedlam. Imagine what they will say when I propose that females be admitted to the clubs! But that is a discussion for some other time. At the moment, we have something far more important to resolve."

She held her breath.

"I needn't waste my breath telling you all my faults and weaknesses, for you have them all down in writing. You also know all my fears in life, and doubts, as well. But there is one thing of which I have no doubt—I want to spend the rest of my life with you. Will you become my wife as well as my best friend, Gus?"

"Oh Alex, I should like it above all things. I think I have been in love with you since the first curse popped out of your mouth." She hugged him very tightly, then looked up and bit her lip. "But I must warn you. I doubt I shall be able to change. You already know I am headstrong, opinionated, and sharp-tongued. And not very obedient."

He couldn't repress a laugh. "I hadn't noticed."

When her own soft laughter had died away, she ventured to speak again. "There is also the matter of Firebrand. Perhaps you would not wish a wife who would insist on writing such incendiary things? For I would, you know. Not even for you could I give up expressing what I believe in."

He became very serious. "You cannot imagine that I would try to prevent you from doing that which is so very much a part of you. Besides, I have quite a fondness for our fiery friend. After all, it was he who introduced us."

"You are not afraid of the sparks that sometimes fly between us?"

"On the contrary. They will keep our marriage from ever burning down into a bed of cold coals. In truth, my love, I cannot conceive of a better match." His mouth took hers in a long, lingering kiss. "Now,